ALSO BY ANNE ARGULA

Homicide My Own

Walla Walla Suite

KRAPP'S LAST CASSETTE

KRAPP'S LAST CASSETTE

INDEX

A

A NOVEL

Anne Argula

BALLANTINE BOOKS · NEW YORK

A Ballantine Books Trade Paperback Original

Copyright © 2009 by Darryl Ponicsan

Published in the United States by Ballantine Books, an imprint of The Random House Publishing Group, a division of Random House, Inc., New York.

BALLANTINE and colophon are registered trademarks of Random House, Inc.

Library of Congress Cataloging-in-Publication Data
Argula, Anne.
Krapp's last cassette : a novel / Anne Argula.
p. cm.
ISBN 978-0-345-49844-1 (pbk.)
e-ISBN 978-0-345-51335-9
1. Screenwriters—California—Los Angeles—Fiction.
2. Abused children—Fiction.   3. Adopted children—Fiction.
4. Family secrets—Fiction.   5. Private investigators—Fiction.   I. Title.
PS3566.O6K73 2009
813'.6—dc22   2008055708

Printed in the United States of America

www.ballantinebooks.com

1 2 3 4 5 6 7 8 9

Book design by Susan Turner

To Cecilia

*"Shall I sing when I am her age, if I ever am? No.
Did I sing as a boy? No. Did I ever sing? No."*

—SAMUEL BECKETT

KRAPP'S LAST CASSETTE

One Saturday Morning in Seattle

To be fair, the new Olympic Sculpture Park had opened to the public just a couple of weeks before, and in the swirl of regional, national, and even international attention, some kinks were yet to be worked out. The charm of the place was that it was more park than art, more an urban refuge than a museum.

An elegant walk, laid out as a gigantic "Z" above both railroad tracks and street, began at street level with the Bill and Melinda Gates Amphitheater. The sculpture park mixed the grand with the simple: huge steel installations just off narrow winding paths spread with wood chips.

Though the park was free during specific hours of operation, it was, in a way, always open: ungated and unfenced. Sandwich signs at various points of ingress and egress were all that indicated the place was closed for the day.

This is not to say there was no security. Not much seemed necessary, since the art itself was too massive to steal without a crane. Security concerns were focused against taggers and vandals and homeless winos. So far, security had been breached only by a neighborhood insomniac, an old pensioner who could not understand why he couldn't walk his Jack Russell terrier on what was obviously an ideal dog walk. He did, after all, clean up after his pet.

That night, with the temperature hovering around twenty-five degrees, both security guards were in the video station watching the monitors. One of them was supposed to be on foot or bicycle patrol, but considering the frigid weather, they spaced those rounds a bit farther apart and instead doubled their efforts in the warm monitoring room.

Sometime around three in the morning, an infrared alarm was tripped. Both guards looked to the screen and saw the old man and his little terrier, pulling at opposite ends of the recoiling leash.

"Dogs don't even like to walk at night," said one of the guards. "They like to sleep at night. Especially when it's cold as this. The poor mutt's gonna freeze his little balls off."

"The old guy probably doesn't know what time it is. Or where he's at. Go tell him to go home."

Put out, the other guard bundled up and left. As he did, another infrared went off. The remaining guard glanced again at the monitor, thinking the old man had doubled back and gone home on his own, or that maybe the dog had circled back on his extending leash. But he didn't see anything.

It wasn't until four hours later—morning now, though still nearly as dark as night—that the foot patrol guard, back in the warm monitoring room, noticed something odd about the *Wandering Rocks* installation (Tony Smith, 1912–1980).

To be fair, again, the guards never paid much attention to the art itself. Their interest was in the grounds. They had scanned the monitors many number of times for the past four hours and must have seen the naked dead body lying on the black steel trapezoid, but somehow their joint subconsciousness had registered it as part of the art. They were seeing it in black and white, after all, and a critic might have argued that the addition of the woman's figure, emerging as it were from the steel, actually enhanced the aesthetics of the piece.

And though unseen, the communion wafer wedged into the vagina of the dead woman might have been considered the artist's signature.

1

Live in Seattle and you learn to layer. I was locked into the first-class can, hurling through the night, thirty thousand feet above Oregon's sleepy charms, struggling to peel off my clothes before spontaneously combusting and turning Alaska Flight 291 into a fiery ball with no direction home. Really, they shouldn't let me through security. If hot flashes were detectable to scanners, a whole demographic, the one that kept *Matlock* on the air for so long, would be grounded for their own safety and the safety of others.

Locking my knees and bracing my hands against the bulkheads, I gave a fleeting moment's thought to all those nameless, shameless shaggers who have at times partied in similar spaces and then bragged to their friends about it. Even in the days when I *was* having sex I wanted it on silk sheets, with some scented candles about, not in a public crapper the size of an upright coffin.

At last I got down to my bra, sweating out enough salt to corrode the plumbing. To be honest with you, the amount of perspiration pumping out of me would have left space in a thimble for my old lieutenant's heart, but it felt like Niagara. I held a handful of paper towels under the faucet, hammering it with my other hand to keep the water flowing. I ran the wet towels over my face and torso and under my arms. I looked at my reflection in the mirror and saw my hair uncurling. I took three deep breaths, and then I took three more. If I had a happy place, I would have gone to it.

In any case, my flamethrowers backed down and reset to safety. Crisis passed. Quinn has once again been defused. We will survive.

And then—how startling and wonderful—a blip broke the flat line that was the sexual me. A twinge. An echo of a feeling long, long forgotten, and I knew why: that man. That man sitting next to me in the first-class cabin. Without drying, I layered my clothes back on and had a serious look at myself. Did I need this? For sure, not. So why did I have this half a fantasy of dragging him in with me and doing the Mile High thing? Oh, what a feeling! Was I ready for the club?

I youksed the door, fighting a small panic of entrapment, before I figured out to accordion the thing and managed to set myself free.

The stewardess, not much younger than I, and maybe a kindred spirit, offered me another Corona. I jumped on it.

I sat down again, next to that man and the slight odor of cloves. We smiled at each other. And, lo, in Little Sahara, falls a dewdrop.

"Here's to it," he said, and tapped his scotch against my beer. "Drinking in the sky."

When we landed in Seattle, my head was on his shoulder, and I was fast asleep.

2

I DON'T LIKE FLYING, WHICH DOESN'T MEAN I PREFER TRAINS, boats, or buses. I don't like to travel, period. As the Zen Buddhists say, why go to distant lands when you have a perfectly good place to sit at home?

Most of us, though, are obliged to do more than sit, and so occasionally even I have to dangle in the air.

First class makes a difference. I'd never flown first class before, but then I'd never flown on anybody else's dime before, either. I was not used to being treated that way, not as a cop, not as a PI, not as a woman.

Early that morning a limo had picked me up at my apartment down in Pioneer Square. It was one of those days when the weight of the cold gray northern sky made it tough even to push open the front door.

The car was waiting for me on Yesler. I tried to get inside without my three Indians noticing. The boys had taken up permanent residence—as permanent as it got for them—

under the pergola across the street. Drunk as they always were, they never missed much of what was happening.

Clifford Everybodytalksabout got to his feet fairly fast and shouted out, "Yo, Quinn, livin' large, baby!"

The other two struggled to get off the bench, using each other for leverage. The singer, David Hidesbehindthesmoke, yelled, "Paris Hilton! It's Paris Hilton!"

"Fuck you," I yelled back pleasantly. "Can I drop you somewhere? Like down a hole?"

They didn't need a second invitation. They staggered across James and Yesler where the streets come together, just managing not to get killed by traffic. I took them to Muscatel Meadows.

"Where're you goin', Quinn?"

"I'm going to Hollywood, baby!" I said, sounding like one of those *American Idol* hopefuls, but in my case the enthusiasm ran false. I didn't want to go anywhere, but I had a cleared desk and I didn't want my bank account to resemble it.

I gave them a ten. They left a pungency behind, and although the driver was cool about it I could tell he saw this as the start of a bad day. Suffer.

So there I was, flying first class, compliments of a heavy-hitting screenwriter with the unfortunate name of Alex Krapp. Later, nearing what I thought was the end of my day with him, after a nice dinner at the Ivy and a bottle of chardonnay, I asked him why, since he was in show business, he hadn't changed his name. He told me he had, and some of the expensive wine flew out of my nose. "You chose Alex Krapp!"

He smiled sheepishly. "I know."

"Nothing wrong with it, but . . ."

"It's kept me from directing. Who'd want to go see 'A Krapp Film'?"

He had called me the day before, at my office, and told me who he was. I mean, he gave me his name, not like he expected me to recognize it, which I didn't. Who remembers the writer's name?

He'd asked me what the weather was like.

"Hot and dusty," I said. He chuckled, sort of.

"Don't you just love the Northwest, Seattle, and the mountains, and the water? And all those islands? Aren't the islands incredible?"

"Yeah, some people like islands. Some people need them. I'm not one of them."

He mumbled something about how true, how true, that some people are drawn to islands.

"I read about you," he said, "in the papers."

I'd recently been involved in a high-profile murder case. It was all over the news up here. When I saw my picture in the *Times* I was like, Da frick, you've let yourself go, girl. Next day, I joined the Seattle Club and worked out every day, pumping iron and going goofy with aerobics. I did detours around Dick's Burgers and lost the number for Belltown Pizza, dining instead on the creatures that swim in the Northwest waters or lie in its mud, some veggies on the side or a salad spritzed with lemon juice. Woi Yesus, I dropped twenty pounds overnight and suddenly I'm getting long eyes from two out of three limp dicks all up and down First Avenue.

"I didn't know that story had gone much beyond the Northwest," I said.

"Lurid travels. Anyway, I found out a little about you," he said.

"You probably got it all."

"I found out that you're kind of in close proximity, sometimes, when people get killed."

Not that his observation wasn't true, but I was about to say something bitchy. The conventional wisdom being that breath is worth saving, I decided I would hit him with a hang-up instead. That last case put me on the map as a PI, which has its downside. I got lots of calls after that, like, You want me to do *what*? Listen, lady, I'm a dog person myself and I do believe that if you're looking for true happiness you could do a lot worse than a warm puppy, but I am not going to find your lost poodle, okay? Cogitating on that, or something, slowed my hand, and Alex Krapp apologized before I could hammer down the phone.

"I'm sorry," he said. "I was being glib. I'm not very good at it."

I Googled him while he was waiting for my reply. The apology sounded sincere. I'd give him another minute to tell me why he was calling and what would be in it for me. Google had twenty-seven thousand, five hundred and forty-two hits on him.

"Mr. Krapp," I said, newly impressed. "Shoot."

"Sorry. Down here in Hollywood before we get to the point there is some necessary schmoozing. You know what that means?"

"Yeah, but I don't schmooze."

"I do. I have to, but, again, I'm not very good at it."

"Yeah, I can see that."

I quickly scanned my computer screen and picked up the titles of some of my favorite movies of the past thirty years.

"Mrs. Quinn, I want to hire you."

The bobber goes down. Now, *that's* what I'm talking about.

"For what?" asked I, because I'm capable of a lot of things and open to most. "And it's just Quinn, okay? No Mrs., Miz, or Miss."

"Could you get on a plane and fly down here, just for the day?"

"No. Where's here?"

"LA. At my expense, of course. First class."

If he had said Phoenix I might have passed, even with all of that sun, but LA was my old stomping grounds and I hadn't been back in years and years. How many years, Johnny? Well, when I was there, an evening's entertainment, when you were broke, was to stroll the length of Hollywood Boulevard, from La Brea to the freeway. People would bring their children and push baby carriages, and say hello to everybody. That was then. Don't do that now. How long ago? A nice apartment just off Sunset, west of La Brea, could be had for less than two hundred bucks.

I had moved to Los Angeles from my parents' row house in Shenandoah, Pennsylvania, hard-coal country. I was part of the inevitable exodus of the younger generation, which left the place pretty much to pensioners and black-lung disability cases. Now, I'm told, the Mexicans are trying to bring the town back to life, though not everybody is happy about that. Free fall is okay, I guess, if you're all speaking the same language as you go down, or at least with similar accents.

People laugh when I tell them why I chose LA as my escape destination, so feel free. It was all because of *Dragnet* reruns.

While other girls my age were enamored of one or another of the Beatles, I had the hots for Sergeant Joe Friday, and wondered what could possibly be more rewarding to gather than just the facts.

My dream was to go to LA and become a dispatcher for the Los Angeles Police Department, at that time recognized as the most efficient, and the least corrupt, police department in the nation. That was then.

The LAPD considered me too young for such responsibility, so I spent the next three years doing what a girl's got to do: selling polyester jumpsuits by day, slinging pizzas by night. But then the LAPD started seriously recruiting minorities and women, and it hit me: My God, I could be a cop. The genuine article. Fuck a whole bunch of dispatchers.

3

I GOT OFF THE PLANE AT LAX UNENCUMBERED EXCEPT FOR my purse, and even that had gone through a quick edit before I left. I wasn't packing my Smith & Wesson LadySmith, for example, without which I felt topless.

A young driver too cute for his own good was waiting for me, holding a white card with my name on it. He led me to another limo and commenced to make some small talk on the way to the Fox lot, where Krapp had his office. The driver wanted to know what slot I filled in the business, the only business that mattered in LA. When I told him I wasn't in the business, he lost all interest. This passenger wouldn't be leaving his car with his screenplay in hand.

At the Fox gate I lowered the window so the guard could have a look at me. He gave the driver directions and soon I was walking down a hallway with movie posters on each side to remind everyone of the long history of quality films produced by Twentieth Century–Fox. That was then.

The name on the door: Krapp Productions. It looked like a gag. I went inside.

The reception area was small, just about big enough for his secretary and her desk, plus a small davy with telephones on the tiny tables at each end. The walls were covered with Krapp's own movie posters, which had pictures of actors who were not stars when the movies were made, but are now: Tom Cruise, Matt Damon, Sean Penn.

"You must be Miss Quinn," said the secretary, who made herself seem to care. She had been behind this or another desk like it for a very long time. She had seen them come and had seen them go, as the saying has it, and she probably wouldn't mind the day when she saw herself go. I knew the type.

"Just Quinn," I said.

She picked up the phone, hit a button, and said, "Miss Quinn is here."

Let us imagine she heard him say, Show her in, because she wearily got to her feet and took the three steps to her left and opened the door for me.

Alex Krapp rose from behind his desk and came forward to greet me. A little something caught in my breath. I didn't expect him to be so . . . I don't know. (To this day.)

He smiled, but he had to dig for it. He was mildly disheveled, overdue for another hundred-dollar haircut, wearing jeans and a maroon cashmere pullover. He was about sixty, youthful in appearance but old for that business. Anyone over fifty is old for that business.

Maybe he carried a few extra pounds, but he was tall and seemed fit. A sadness had taken root in him, a cosmic dread. His face was long and his eyes were long, and in them there was longing. His was, I imagined, a hard face to live with, whatever side of it you were on. I can't explain what he had, but it put the cuffs on me.

Don't jump to conclusions—it wasn't love at first sight. I'm smarter than that. (Though nobody can outsmart love.) But it was *something* at first sight, I don't know what: a catching of the breath, a little hurt where there was no wound. Save for one drunken mercy mission, I hadn't had a man nor wanted one since I'd first learned my ex was diddling his pharmacist's assistant while I was pulling overtime with the Spokane PD.

He shook my hand and he held it for what seemed like a long moment. Then he looked down at my hand and scanned my face in an odd way. I felt like I was being examined.

"Would you like something to drink? Coffee, water, a Coke?"

I've been told you should take something when offered, that it makes people feel better, so I said, "A coffee with a bit of milk in it would be nice."

It would be the hardest thing his secretary would have to do that day.

More posters were on the walls inside his office, this time the grown-ups: Jack Nicholson, Barbra Streisand, Harrison Ford.

"Please, sit down. How was your flight?"

The place looked like what a writer's office ought to look like. Writing work got done in there. A laptop sat on one small table and an old upright typewriter on another. On his large oak desk was a coffee mug full of sharpened pencils, a bowl full of M&M's, a lamp, lots of paper, and a framed photo of a boy, maybe twelve years old, goofy-looking, with a wide grin. Next to the old typewriter was a picture of the screenwriter in leathers, atop a chromed-up Harley-Davidson motorcycle.

I sat on an overstuffed davy. A Navajo throw covered most of the back of it. He sat across the distressed coffee table on a brown leather easy chair. When the secretary came in with my coffee, he introduced her to me as Gwendolyn.

"I think I'll have a cup of tea, Gwendolyn. The vervain."

Only I saw the look, when she turned, like: He could have told me that in the first place.

"So," he said. "Thank you for coming. I know it makes it a long day, flying down and back, and not knowing what for, but I think by the time we're done here, you'll understand why I had to meet you in person."

"Mr. Krapp . . . and by the way, I've seen most of your movies, and I liked them."

"A satisfied customer. Thank you. And call me Alex, please."

"It's a pleasure to meet you, and I'm figuring you must really need the services of a private detective to fly one in, but I'm wondering why you don't get one down here. The woods are full of 'em."

He chuckled, like a little cough, like a person would who isn't used to it. His upper teeth were all capped and white. His lowers were whitened to a pretty good match.

"This is LA—there aren't any woods for them to hide in." His face went serious again. "I'd prefer not to require a private detective . . ."

"That's the general preference."

". . . but I guess it's come to that."

"Again, why not get a local?"

"A couple reasons. One is that there are no secrets in Hollywood, only true rumors. Another is the . . . issue."

"And the issue is?"

"We'll get to that."

I quoted him my rich guy rate, top of the sliding scale. He didn't twitch. I learned later that his own fee, for writing a screenplay, whether it became a movie or not, was a cool million. I learned at the same time that all screenwriters look sad.

"Have you ever found a missing person?" he asked.

"Oh yeah," I said without hesitation.

If I had a résumé it would list only two, and one of those was found dead and not actually by me. So the truth was, I found one, an anorexic teenage girl from Kirkland who wanted only to go somewhere where a daily tomato and a single walnut would be considered a well-balanced diet. That *somewhere* turned out to be a mattress on the cellar floor in a crash pad in Capitol Hill.

The screenwriter turned the framed photo toward me.

"I want you to find this boy," he said.

"Okay," said I. I opened my notebook. "Your son?"

"In a manner of speaking."

"What manner would that be?"

"I love him like a son."

I had the feeling that Alex Krapp didn't use the word *love* easily. Like maybe he'd used it three times in his life and two of them he wished he hadn't.

"Adopted?"

"Yes, but not by me. Not officially."

"What's his name?" I asked.

"Danny . . . Daniel Alex Timpkins."

"Alex. Like you."

"He took my name."

"Why?"

"Because he considers me another father."

"Who's the other one?"

"We'll get to that."

The things we would have to get to were stacking up.

I took another look at the picture.

"Do you have any children of your own?" I asked. Any wife? I didn't ask.

"I do. I have two, both grown now. I was never the father I should have been, to either of them. The pressures of this kind of work, the travel, the drinking, the temptations, the two divorces . . . all of that. Danny is another chance. My last chance."

"How old is the boy?"

"Fifteen. The picture's a few years old."

"You don't have a recent one?"

"No."

"Why not?"

"We'll get to that."

Stacking up.

"Have you notified the police?" I asked.

"No."

"Why not?"

"I can't."

"Will we get to why? Later?"

"Yes."

"Is the boy a runaway?"

"No, far from it."

"Do you have another picture?"

He opened his desk drawer and gave me a wallet-size copy of the photo on his desk. He looked at it again with his long sad eyes.

"When and where was he last seen?"

He hesitated. "Let's say Seattle."

"Which is why you called me, ain't?"

He nodded.

"When?" I asked.

"What?"

"When was he last seen in Seattle?"

"That takes a little explanation. I don't know where to start."

"Take your time."

"Danny is an incredible boy. A prodigy. A genius, really. He plays guitar and keyboard, self-taught. He can speak Spanish fluently. He writes and draws—and I mean he does both well, professionally. He has a photographic memory. And, God, he's courageous. He's got more heart than you'll ever encounter in another human being."

"My son can swim pretty good. He's in the Navy." I got another smile out of him. "When did Danny go missing?"

"Let me start at the beginning." Alex Krapp looked like he was feeling his way for how this scenario should open. FADE IN: Now what? "HBO wanted me to do something for them."

"Cable television? Home Box Office?"

"Right. That was the true beginning. They'd been after me for some time, but they don't pay very well, so you look for something to do there that you can't do as a feature film."

4

BEFORE HE COULD TELL ME MORE, GWENDOLYN CAME IN with his tea. He waited until she left the room. Whatever he was going to tell me, he hadn't told her, which didn't necessarily mean that she didn't know. Secretaries wind up knowing everything.

"A little over a year ago," he said, "I was on my way to LAX to fly to New York. I'd been meeting with Dustin Hoffman there, off and on, for the past few years, developing a project. Sometimes he meets me out here, sometimes I meet him in New York. We'll probably never do the project, not together. I mean, this happened once before: meet with Dustin for a few years, he never says yes, and then Harrison Ford does the movie and Dustin enjoys the irony that he did more research into the character than the actor who actually played the part. Which in that case wasn't so tough. Harrison Ford is the Robert Mitchum of his generation. Working with Dustin is a lot of fun, though, and you never know, a great movie might come out of it, so I do it. It's time-consuming and expensive, but so is diamond mining."

"Is this about Dustin Hoffman?"

"No."

"Diamond mining?"

"No."

"Harrison Ford?"

"God, no. I'm just pegging the time, the circumstances."

Gwendolyn buzzed him. Krapp looked a tad put out, like even his own secretary doesn't listen to him. He had told her to hold all calls.

"What is it?" he said.

"Danny's on the phone," said the secretary.

Alex Krapp cocked his head at me. "I'll put him on the speakerphone."

"Ask him where he is," I said. "It'll make my job easier."

He put his finger to his lips. He opened a desk drawer and attached a suction cup to the receiver and started a micro-recorder.

"Hey, Danny, how're you doing?"

"The best I can. How're you doing, Poppa?"

"Hanging in. Working."

"I'm sorry to bother you."

"Get out of here, you're no bother."

"It's just that I've been thinking a lot."

"Hello? You're always thinking a lot."

The kid giggled. His voice was frail but with a lilt of the street to it. I could picture him in a hoodie and baggy pants, with a skateboard. He sounded like he hadn't yet done the postpuberty drop. In the chorus he'd be an alto. I would soon learn that he loved to sing. As for Alex Krapp, a brightness came over his face that wasn't there before.

"Do you have me on the speakerphone?"

"Yeah. Is it okay?"

"Is someone with you?"

"Yeah, a hot babe."

The kid giggled. Me, I flushed.

"You want me to pick up? I can hear you just fine."

"No, it's all right."

"So what have you been thinking about?"

"The world doesn't like to hear bad things."

"What do you mean, Danny?"

"People just don't like to believe what stuff can happen to a kid, especially to a blue-eyed, blond kid."

"A kid like you."

"I mean, I can't handle the idea that I'm laying my heart out and that people won't believe me. That's what those people always used to say, before, that nobody would ever believe me anyway so I'd better keep my mouth shut until they told me to open it."

Krapp looked at me. "Your parents, you mean?"

"Sperm donor and the incubator."

Krapp pursed his lips.

"You believe in me, don't you, Poppa?"

"You don't have to ask. You know I do. Everything starts with today."

"I trust you, you know. You're one of the few."

"We'll get past this."

I wondered what *this* was.

The kid went on: "I just don't want to set myself up to be hurt anymore. I've been rushing you to push ahead with this project, because I wanted to be around to see it. Only now, I don't know. I have to save energy, and trying to preserve my dignity just sucks it up."

"I know, Danny, it's a bitch. But it's not your fight. Let me deal with this. You know what your fight is."

Their voices alone told me that something very heavy was on them, but I had no idea what.

The kid said, "There was a time when I cried about being lonely. Now there are times when loneliness might just suit me fine."

"No, you'll never be lonely again."

"I'll always have you, won't I, Poppa?"

"Always. We're a team."

"Thanks, Poppa. Talking to you always makes me feel better. I had a bad night again. I spiked a fever."

"How high?"

"Hundred 'n six."

"Jesus."

"Vic had to put me on ice. Going into a tub of ice water is like, I don't know, flying through outer space."

"Where's he get all the ice?"

"At the gas station on the corner. He's their biggest ice customer. They should deliver." The kid giggled again and his voice went higher. "I'm sorry to call you in the morning, Poppa. I know you write in the mornings."

"Hey, I told you—you can call me anytime."

"I'll let you go now. Just hearing your voice gives me a boost."

"You don't get off that easy." Krapp nodded his head to me. Like, Get this. "I want a song."

"Okay. Name it."

" 'American Pie.' "

The kid started singing in his small squeaky voice— *"Long, long time ago . . ."*—and he didn't stop until he finished that ton of a song, written before he was born.

"Now you've given *me* a boost," said the screenwriter.

They hung up saying they loved each other, in that familial way you do.

I closed my notebook. I'd just seen my case go out the window, so I wondered what plane I'd be catching back to Seattle, and away from any other possibilities.

"Sounds like a nice kid," I said.

"One in a million. That little guy has changed my life."

"Used to be, recording phone conversations was illegal in California," I told him.

"Our little secret, okay? Danny is terminal. I need to remember him, every word."

"He's dying?"

Alex Krapp nodded. I knew the weight now.

I wasn't a cop anymore. Let him record his phone conversations.

"Where was I?" Alex Krapp asked the ceiling.

I answered, "Does it matter? Sounds like the kid is no longer missing."

"Oh, but he is."

"He's missing but he's not missing?"

"In a manner of speaking."

That again. Some people are good at holding two contradictory ideas in their minds at the same time. I'm not one of them.

"Maybe you should call for the car now," I said. A dying boy who is missing, but not really? I didn't see a future in it.

"Hear me out, Quinn. I need you."

Well, gentlemen, that's all you have to say to a woman to keep her from going out the door. Most men won't, though. Or can't.

He called Gwendolyn for a refill on my coffee and I

leaned back. "Okay," I said. "You're on your way to the airport, to go to New York, to meet with Dustin Hoffman, who has nothing to do with this story."

"And I get a call from Robert Henshaw, the head of HBO. He tells me he's found a project that might interest me. It's a book, a memoir written by a fourteen-year-old boy."

"A fourteen-year-old boy has enough to put in a memoir?"

"That's what I said to Robert. What the hell does a kid that age have to write about? He told me that the kid has AIDS, TB, and a slew of other things that are going to kill him. The boy is terminal, has only months to live. So he had to get it all down. At this point I don't know the details, only that this kid has been put through unimaginable abuse by his parents and he had to get it down on paper before he died. I liked that. And here's the thing: what he put down was not just about the abuse and the pain and suffering. He wrote about hope. The little bits of goodness he was able to find in a life of horror."

"I'm impressed."

"So was I, but I told Robert, I don't know, a dying little boy? Sexual abuse? AIDS?"

"Who wants to watch that?"

"Exactly. And what writer wants to live with that for a year or so. But I *always* try to talk myself out of a project when I first hear it. It's so much easier to say no. Everybody does. Executives, directors, stars, even writers. You start off thinking you don't want to do something, then you inch up on it, or it inches up on you, and before you know it you're already doing it in your head, and you can't talk yourself out of it anymore."

I knew a little bit about that.

"And the boy, of course, was Danny, the kid I just heard on the speakerphone."

"Yes, but we're ahead of ourselves," he said.

"Sorry. Go on."

"I agreed to read the book. Robert said he would have it delivered to me at LAX. I hung back from security for twenty minutes and a messenger arrived with the book. I took it on the plane and read it on the flight to New York. I intended to read the opening chapter, have a drink, and go to sleep, but I read the whole thing. It wasn't exactly a masterpiece. It had all the pitfalls you'd expect from even a very bright fourteen-year-old. It was amateurish, but, damn, it was like a kick in the heart. As soon as I got off the plane at Kennedy I called Robert and said I'd do it. I considered it a moral imperative. I wanted this kid's story to reach a mass audience. You know where his story took place."

"Sure. Seattle. That's why I'm here."

5

As an LAPD cop, I'd dealt with rich Hollywood dudes, bullies who when oily charm wouldn't cut it resorted to threats and insults. I'd encountered the broken and the badly bent, ready to eat the gun but for the fear of what that might do to the face, and I'd run up against the smarmy morons who hit the jackpot with the eighth remake of a comic book, and so equated money with brains and arrogance with charisma, and I'd seen the beautiful young women in their fuck-me high heels who encouraged the morons in their delusions.

Alex Krapp was not like any of them. He was on the sweet and gentle side, and the sadness in his eyes bore no relationship to the opening weekend grosses. He told me Danny's story in wavering tones, disappointed in a God who would let it happen, if He could have stopped it.

"To anyone on the street," he said, "Danny's parents looked like your basic set. They dressed well, they spoke well, they had legitimate jobs. They walked like normal human beings. That's where the similarity ended. Just below their ordinary surfaces, they were monsters, these people.

"They made their son sleep in the garage, on a mover's blanket, in an old refrigerator box. He had a small cardboard box with a change of clothes, a few pictures, a sketchbook. He had no winter coat. No raincoat, either, in a famously wet climate. He had no toys, nor books. They gave him only enough food to stay alive. They knocked him around almost daily. It gets worse. They made him watch sexual acts and then forced him to do those acts with them and their friends. Then, they put him in kiddie porn movies."

I twitched a little, but I kept quiet. He could see my discomfort.

"The amazing thing is that all of that would have been bearable to Danny. He told me he could have taken it, he could have found a way, if only they would show, in some small way, that they cared about him.

"School included a free breakfast and all the books he could read, so he loved going there. It gave him a safe place, a refuge, and he was an excellent student, especially for one whose cardinal rule was not to call attention to himself. He had a best friend at school, another boy named Perry. Perry lent him sweatshirts that he could layer on against the cold and the rain. He became a source of aspirin and even antibiotics against the pain and sickness that dogged Danny even then.

"All of this misery, all of this horror, though, was only background for Danny's story. He looked to the future. He dreamed that someday he would play center field for the Mariners. *Someday* became his favorite word, his mantra. The title of his book is *Someday I'll Find It*. Perry kept pressing him to do something, to call somebody, but Danny had

had it drilled into him that no one would ever believe him. His misery would only become worse if he made any trouble for his parents or their friends.

"So instead Danny would draw pictures of Kermit the Frog and sing to himself, *'Someday we'll find it, the rainbow connection, the lovers, the dreamers, and me . . .'* "

Alex Krapp actually sang for me, in a ragged but not un-pleasant voice. It came so naturally to him I was sure he had sung it often with the boy. I was right.

"Danny's father would hold him by the ankles out of a second-story window and threaten to drop him. He told him that no one would ever notice he wasn't around anymore."

"When did he do that?" I asked. "I mean, what would tip him over?"

"It could happen at any time, but it was sure to happen whenever the school nurse called home saying that Danny was sick and should see a doctor. But he doesn't dwell on these things. He tells funny little stories of school and teach-ers and unexpected kindnesses. He describes childhood ad-ventures he and Perry used to have on the streets of Seattle. He fantasized the life he might someday live. Why couldn't it happen that some kind man, some big man with principles could find him and protect him from his parents? Perry kept telling him they would kill him soon. Because each day things got worse.

"Then one day they forced him to stay home from school to vacuum the house and do the laundry. The denial of that one day of school tipped him. The little guy managed to pick up the heavy vacuum machine and throw it through the TV screen. He flung the laundry across the living room and took off, heading for the waterfront. He was going to jump and put an end to his false hopes. He was worn out from constant pain and fever.

"He stood with his hands in his pockets looking over the rail to the icy water below. A cutting wind sliced across the Sound."

"This is from his book, right?"

"Yeah. That's how he described it. He was about to jump, when he noticed a poster taped around a light pole: NEED HELP? It was for a hotline, for people in crisis. Danny had a dime and three nickels and three pennies in his pocket. He took out the three pennies and threw them into the murky water. He thought he might as well put the other coins into a phone and tell somebody that once there was a boy named Danny. That's all he had left to do.

"He found a public phone at the ferry landing. A woman named Celeste answered. She spoke in a soft slow voice. She asked for his name, if he wanted to tell it to her. He told her his name, and she kept him talking and said that if he jumped into Puget Sound one of two things would happen as a result: Something would become nothing, or he would make God very disappointed. And who knows what that might lead to?"

"She said that?"

"Something like that."

"Danny talked to her for an hour: about what his life was like, about his abusive parents, and how he could not take it any longer and there was no way in the world he could ever go home now. She told him he should not go home. She *insisted* he not go home, and this hit Danny like a lifeline.

"He asked her what he was supposed to do—he didn't see any options. His father would kill him if he didn't kill himself. Celeste said in a calm voice, 'Neither of those things is going to happen, because he loses his power now that you've walked away.' She started to describe a lot of the very things Danny had been through, without all the finer details, and she knew exactly the words that his father and mother used to control him. He was stunned. For the first time he realized that he was not the only one.

"Celeste asked him to join her for hot chocolate at Starbucks on First Avenue and Marion, which was nearby. Danny was still inclined to jump, but hot chocolate was an unimaginable treat. He went to the Starbucks and waited outside in the cold for the woman to show up.

"She arrived at Starbucks with an older man named Bob, a retired Army officer who was a new volunteer, someone she was breaking in. In his book Danny describes Celeste as having raven hair—a beautiful woman, warm and comforting. While the three of them were talking and having the delicious hot chocolate with whipped cream on top, she reached over and felt his forehead. Her touch was soft and comforting.

"She knew right away that he had a fever. He said that he usually had a fever and that he lived on stolen aspirins. She asked him when he last saw a doctor. He told her he'd never seen a doctor, nor a dentist. She asked him if he had any marks on his body, any bruises or scars. Danny was embarrassed by that, but she finally got it out of him. He pointed to the corners of his eyes where he had two scars deliberately inflicted by his father. He told her that he had others, elsewhere, and lots of bruises below the neck.

"You're not going back there, she said. He told her he didn't want to, but he knew they would find him if he didn't. She asked for his trust and promised to protect him.

"She and Bob took him to the emergency room of a hospital, and then called social services and the police. Bob and the police went to Danny's house and saw how he was forced to live in the garage. They arrested his father on the spot. His mother wasn't there and his father claimed not to know her whereabouts. The father would eventually go to prison, but the mother was never seen again.

"Bob came back to the hospital with Danny's box of belongings. He and Celeste sat in his hospital room. As sick as he was, Danny could see an attraction between them, and it made him feel better. He said that he felt like Cupid. Bob was a big man, confident and powerful. Danny knew his father would be afraid of this man.

"Over the next few days, while Danny was undergoing medical tests, Bob and Celeste waited together in the hospital. They fell in love.

"Eventually the doctor came to them and told them that Danny was a very sick boy. He was malnourished, anemic, and he suffered the effects of aspirin poisoning. What's more, he had thirty-six untreated broken bones, and they found several needle fragments lodged in his scrotum. And he was in the second stage of syphilis. Celeste fainted.

"He spent the next six weeks in the hospital, where they brought him back to a better level of health, though they had to remove his spleen in the process.

"During this time Celeste decided to adopt Danny. Bob got down on one knee in the hospital waiting room and asked Celeste to marry him; they would raise the boy together. She said yes.

"Before all that could become official, when Danny was discharged both he and Bob went to live with Celeste and her two daughters from a previous marriage, Jenny and Leslie.

The two girls moved into one bedroom and Danny was given his own room, for the first time in his life. Bob slept on the sofa.

"Their first dinner together, Danny was afraid to sit at the table—he had never sat at a table for dinner. They persuaded him to sit, but he was afraid to eat. Pasta and vegetables and salad and fruit covered the table. He stared at it all in wonder. They managed to get him to eat some pasta and a little fruit. Came bedtime, he was too frightened to sleep in the bed. For the first few nights he slept on the floor.

"Bob and Celeste got married and managed through connections to get a quick adoption of Danny. His father went to prison and his mother was a fugitive. The new family should have lived happily ever after. But they didn't. Danny grew more and more tired, and he was having respiratory problems. He went back to the hospital. The diagnosis was AIDS. Just around the same time, Bob was called back into the Army and sent to Iraq. Danny developed TB and had to spend a good deal of his time in an oxygen tent. Doctors thought he probably had less than six months to live."

The story was hurting my stomach. "So he must be in a hospital now somewhere, ain't?" I asked.

"There's more to the story."

"Okay."

"One day Danny was sitting up on his hospital bed and reading. This tough Italian guy comes into his room and looks at his chart. His name was Vic and he wore a Harley-Davidson leather jacket. Turns out he was an old classmate of Celeste's. He spoke gruffly and seemed not to care about anything, but Danny could see through that. He looked at the chart and said, 'So you got AIDS. No big deal. I got it too.' Danny was surprised. The guy looked pretty healthy. 'It's the other stuff we got to get you past,' said Vic. Danny did not miss the *we*. 'Says you fight them when they try to take your temperature.' Danny didn't say anything. 'It's the up-the-ass thing, right?' Danny still didn't say anything. 'You like this place?' the guy asked. 'I hate it here,' said Danny. 'Well, then, let's get your butt home where it belongs,' said Vic.

"Vic happened to be a doctor. Doctor Victor D'Amato. He discharged Danny from the hospital and moved with him into Celeste's house, sleeping on the sofa and living off the rental of his own house. Because of his own health status, his practice had practically disappeared, so he gave it up and attended to Danny exclusively. That around-the-clock medical and emotional attention is what's keeping Danny alive. That and his own spirit, his incredible will to live."

6

At times, as he told Danny's story, Alex Krapp would rest his chin on his hand or he would stand, stretch, and move about his office. Once or twice I stood up and leaned over the back of the davy. It was a hard story to hear.

Telling it wearied him, and I have to admit I kind of wanted to lie down myself. What was sapping me, beyond the gut-wrench of the story alone, were the similarities between Danny's story and what happened to Randy Merck.

"Do you remember reading anything about a guy named Randy Merck?" I asked him.

"Who?"

"Randy Merck. He was one of the principals in that case, the one that brought me to your attention. The one you read about."

"The guy who . . . ?"

"Yeah, that guy. Well, Randy, as a boy, was rented out to pedophiles by his father."

"Really?"

"Yeah, and his father was busted and sent to prison. I interviewed him on McNeil Island. And in that case, too, the mother disappeared."

"But wouldn't that have been years ago?"

"Twenty, easy. Randy turned out to be a serial rapist."

"Not surprising. What's wonderful about Danny is that he didn't turn out to be a monster."

"Here's the kicker, though. Randy's father also pushed pins and needles up into his scrotum."

"Jesus . . . I never heard of such a thing till Danny."

"All those details. Can't be a coincidence."

The screenwriter sat back silently, his head down, as though he had an answer he wasn't yet willing to propose. I couldn't let it go.

"Unless it shows some kind of generational pattern, established methods," I said. "Some kind of ritual abuse."

He raised his head. "Do you know anything about that?"

"Not yet."

"We can talk more about that," he said. "After lunch. You hungry?"

"I could eat."

I could always eat but he didn't have to know that.

"We can order sandwiches in, or would you rather go out for lunch? Or we could just walk over to the lot commissary."

"I could use the air and the walk."

I'd always pictured studio commissaries as places where movie stars and extras in costume would come on their lunch break.

Studio commissaries used to compete with each other over the quality of their food. It was just one more element that attracted talent. That was then. I mean, no complaints, I enjoyed a serviceable Cobb salad, but the place itself was something of a letdown, just a hurried gathering of suits and working stiffs. All of its character was in the walls, and even they were fading.

Over lunch Krapp said, "Tell me about your own story."

"It's a short subject. Born and raised in hardscrabble coal country, ran away to here, to join the LAPD."

"You were an LA cop? I had no idea. What made you leave?"

"I married a pharmacist and moved to his hometown, Spokane. I joined the police force there. Once, I helped my partner solve his own murder from a previous life. My husband left me for a younger woman. I escaped to Seattle, where I became a PI. Ta-da! Now you know my whole story."

His eyes went wide. "Solve his own murder from a previous life?"

"Yeah, I slipped it in there. That's a separate story, and a lot longer. I only mention it because it was a turning point for me. Not only for what happened afterward. It kind of took the pressure off. If I don't get it right this time, I can always work on it next time, but—"

"In your next life?"

I nodded. "But the idea is to get it right this time so you can break the endless cycle of rebirth, which, you know, is no picnic when you stop to think about it."

"And wind up where?" he asked.

"I don't know. Maybe heaven, maybe Harrisburg."

"I'm going to tell you something I learned from Danny."

He made it sound like a secret.

"I've always believed," he said, "that the end of life is the end of everything: what once was is no more. Nothing else made sense to me. Certainly not sitting around in a place called *heaven* for eternity. The other concepts of rebirth or returning to the life force were nice, and almost sounded reasonable except for one thing."

"What?"

"A conscious awareness that it's happened at all. Otherwise, what's the point? What do you learn from coming back as someone, or something, else unless you are aware of doing it? How can you correct your mistakes from your previous life if you're not aware of them?"

"That's always bothered me a little, too. What did you learn from Danny?"

"He's had several near-death experiences. I mean, to the edge and over the edge. During one of those experiences, he remembered."

"Remembered what? A previous life?"

"Not exactly. He remembered being born."

"Hello? Being born?"

"The actual moment. He said it was like coming out of a general anesthetic. He had no idea how long he'd been out, only that he was awake again. He had full consciousness of who he was—or had been; he knew his own name, he looked for his wife and children, he tried to talk. But he discovered he was a *baby*. He realized that he was a man waking up as a baby. He couldn't talk; all he could do was cry. Shortly, he came to accept what was happening. At last he knew the truth, the eternal secret, which he could tell everyone, just as soon as he learned how to talk. He said to himself, This is my new mother, my new father. They are speaking English. They seem happy with me. But every time he tried to say something all he could do was cry.

"With each hour that passed, he let go of more of his previous life and memories, until after a few days he forgot it all. He truly entered into his new life, which would turn out to be with parents who were monsters, but by that time he couldn't remember what he had done that was so wrong, that was so bad to deserve the new life he was in. Though he fights to live, his memory of being born accounts for his lack of fear about dying. He wants to live as long as he can now, because he has so many people who love him and want him to live. He tells me, simply, that he's having too good a time to die. As sick as he is, and in so much pain."

7

WE BOTH HAD DIET COKES. WE SAT SIPPING THEM THROUGH straws, silent for a moment but for the rattling of the ice. Then finally Alex Krapp went back to his story.

"I was in New York, that time, for about a week," he said.

"Meeting with Dustin Hoffman?"

"Mostly. Those meetings go six, eight hours a day."

"Like this one, huh?"

"It all takes time."

"You're in New York for a week," I prompted.

"Robert at HBO calls Danny's mother and tells her they've got me to do the adaptation. He tells her my credits and she tells the kid and they're happy with everything. The evening before I'm supposed to fly back to LA, I get a call from the kid's agent. I didn't know her, but apparently in the book world she drafts a lot of water. She was pleasant and congratulatory, telling me what a wonderful experience this was going to be for me. She adored Danny and was sure I would, too."

"And you did."

"I did. I do. He means the world to me. Everybody loves Danny. The agent urged me to work fast so that Danny would still be alive to read the screenplay. I said I would do my best. She asked me how I planned to work—have I done true stories before, what would my approach be, stuff like that. I said I would start by spending some time with the boy. She stopped me right there and told me that, unfortunately, that wasn't possible. He was too sick and so susceptible to everything that no one was allowed to see him but his mother, who had to go to extraordinary prophylactic lengths to keep him germ-free. He was, essentially, the boy in the bubble. In that case, I said, I would probably start with his school, talk to his teachers and some of his friends. You won't talk to anybody, she snapped at me. You'll work from the book and that's it. I said, 'Look, lady, you don't tell me how to work.' Well, it turned into an argument and I hung up on her. I called Robert and told him we were off to a bad start; I was having second thoughts about going ahead if I couldn't do any research on my own, gather my own insights into the character, and so on.

"The next morning at seven o'clock New York time, my room phone at the Sherry-Netherland wakes me up. It was the boy's adoptive mother. Celeste. She had this soft, soothing voice, both motherly and a little sexy. Robert had told her about my conversation with the agent and had told her where I was staying in New York. She felt she had to call me and explain. People who meet Danny tend to be very protective of him, she said, because they know that in his whole short lifetime no one ever was. We talked for a while and I liked her. I could feel her spirit, her deep devotion. She said it was true that Danny couldn't see anyone. Even her own two daughters had to move out of the house and go live with an uncle. Several times she thought she was losing Danny and it was only the quick actions of Vic, the doctor who lived with them, that kept him alive to fight another day. Danny's whole life was restricted to his room: his computer, his TV, his guitar, his sketchbooks. On rare sunny days he might be able to sit in a chaise in the backyard for half an hour. And of course there were the trips to the emergency room when Danny spiked a fever that even immersion in a bathtub of ice couldn't bring down, or when his lungs filled with fluid, or when his migraines made them afraid that he was having another stroke."

"The kid had a stroke?"

Alex Krapp nodded. "And when I first met him, his T-cell count was at one. One single T cell. We used to joke about it. We named it Horace."

"When you met him?"

"On the telephone."

"So you've never met him face-to-face?"

"No."

Another screenwriter stopped by the table and shook hands with Alex Krapp. They asked each other what they were working on, and they answered each other in vague terms: a project at Universal, a project for HBO, a rewrite for Ridley Scott, a polish for Sydney Pollack. Krapp introduced me as a friend but I've forgotten the name of the other screenwriter, which apparently is the curse of screenwriters everywhere: nobody remembers their names.

Krapp tried to pick up the thread again but again he was interrupted, this time by an attractive woman in her forties. He stood and embraced her and introduced me to Linda Fiorentino. I recognized her from one of Krapp's movies. It's silly, I know, but my first thought was that even though she looked tough, I could drop her with one punch.

It looked like we would not be able to carry on our conversation in the commissary. We had finished our lunch anyway, so we strolled back to his office, talking as we walked. He talked, I listened. He continued to tell me about that first phone call, from the boy's mother, when he thought he might not write the adaptation because of the unpleasant interference from the agent.

"Danny was so excited when we told him you were going to do the script," the mother said to Alex Krapp.

"She told me that the kid had seen all my movies, all that were on DVD or videotape, and he was just thrilled that I would be doing his story. 'We haven't told him that you might not,' she said. 'Every bit of bad news can trigger a physical setback.' Her voice was getting to me. It was so damn comfortable I found myself lost in it. I said, 'Well, I haven't shut the door on it. I really loved his book, the spirit of it, but when an agent starts barking orders at me . . .' She told me she noticed, too, that the agent was a bit overbearing, but she was sure she meant well. She told me I could do this however I wanted to, with full cooperation from her, her husband Vic, anyone I wanted to talk to, and if they could get Danny healthy enough, even for a short time, I would be the first person to visit him. I thanked her for that and she said, 'Would you like to talk to him?' I just then realized that they were on West Coast time, which made it a little after four in the morning for them."

We were about to cross the street to his office when a new black Mercedes stopped in front of us, blocking our way. The tinted window came down on the passenger side and Richard Dreyfuss leaned toward us. He flashed his famous smile and said something to Alex Krapp that I didn't catch. Alex made a quick introduction and said, "New car?"

"Yeah, you like it?" said the actor. "Warner Brothers bought it for me."

It was hard for me to grasp. Down here, your boss might give you a new Mercedes, something you could well afford yourself, just to stay on your good side. Up where I live, the most I ever got was a lukewarm latte because somebody had one extra.

Going up the stairs to the third floor, I said something to Krapp about how much I liked Richard Dreyfuss in *Jaws*.

"That's the movie that ended the Golden Age of Hollywood. After that, everything rode on the opening weekend. Movies became horse races for the artists and carnival rides for the audience. Soon even your mother knew the grosses."

We settled in again back in his office. He didn't know my mother.

8

"NIGHTS ARE BAD FOR DANNY," SAID THE SCREENWRITER. "They became bad for me. He needs someone to put him to sleep, just like a small child, someone to sing to him or tell him a story or just talk until he manages to drop off."

"He's fifteen now?" I asked.

"Yes, but emotionally he's still a small frightened child. Three hours after he's put to sleep, he wakes up from a nightmare and someone has to try to lull him to sleep again."

"When you say *someone* you mean his mother?"

"Or Vic, the live-in doctor. Lately, it's me. He calls me up and tries to act brave. He makes some little joke, but then he'll ask me to hold him."

"Hold him?"

He nodded. "I'll say, 'I'm holding you now, Danny, I've got you in my arms. You're safe. You don't have to be afraid of anything. I'm a big man and I'll protect you against anyone.' Sometimes I sing a song."

"What song?"

"We have two favorites. He always sings the one and I sing the other, or we sing them together. He sings 'Begin the Beguine' and I sing 'McArthur Park.' "

"The one with the cake left out in the rain and he's lost the recipe and doesn't think he can bake it again?"

"That's the one. Worst song ever written. But it cracks him up so we sing it a lot. When we hit the climax—'Oh, no!'—we fall down laughing."

"And he goes back to sleep?"

"Yes. I can always feel it in his voice, when he's dropping off. I just hold the phone until Celeste or Vic picks it up. They check to make sure it's me. Sometimes we talk for a while. Then we say good night. Until he wakes up again."

" 'Begin the Beguine,' that's like, what, from the forties."

"Nineteen thirty-five. He loves all those old songs. And poetry, wow. During one of our early conversations he recited for me the whole of 'The Love Song of J. Alfred Prufrock.' "

"That's a long poem, is it?"

"A hundred and thirty-one lines."

He stared at something I couldn't see, above his head, and said, " 'I grow old . . . I grow old . . .' "

"Everybody does," said I, stupidly.

"No, it's from the poem. 'I grow old . . . I grow old . . . /I shall wear the bottoms of my trousers rolled./Shall I part my hair behind? Do I dare to eat a peach?/I shall wear white flannel trousers, and walk upon the beach./I have heard the mermaids singing, each to each./I do not think they will sing to me.' "

"He knew a poem like that, by heart?"

"Dozens of poems, just as long. But I'm getting ahead of myself again. I was telling you about the first time I had ever talked to him, four a.m. Seattle time, me in New York. He had a weak, fragile voice. He sounded much younger than he really was."

"I noticed that, too."

"He's never passed into puberty, because of all his illnesses. He's fifteen and only about five feet tall. He weighs less than a hundred pounds."

"You've seen pictures?"

"No, none current. He doesn't want any taken. He's embarrassed. All the pictures I have of him are from when he was not so sick. That first time we talked, it wasn't really much about my doing the screenplay. I'm sure I told him I loved the book."

"Well, yeah, you were going to adapt it."

"I've adapted books I didn't love, believe me. I adapted a couple I didn't even like. Oddly enough, that can make for a good movie. Everybody involved may hate the book but love the idea. Anyway, we talked about other things, like music and literature. We talked about things he liked. Food, for instance. He loves pasta. We talked about how some shapes of pasta taste better than others, even though they're made of the same stuff. He's a vegetarian."

Again, I thought about Randy Merck, the serial rapist. He was a vegetarian, too.

"We must have talked for about twenty minutes that first time, and a real connection was made. I mean, damn, I was already racked knowing the kid didn't have long to live. He was very respectful. Called me 'Mr. Krapp,' and 'sir.' When his mother got back on the phone, she told me that he is very wary with people. He'd been hurt so badly in the past, his greatest fear now that he was safe, with people who loved him, was that he would be abandoned. She warned me, really, that if I were to be talking to him it required a certain commitment and responsibility. That said, she urged me to do the screenplay. They would give me full cooperation. I said that I wanted to, just keep that agent out of my hair. Not a problem, she assured me. And it wasn't. I never heard from the agent again."

I said, "So you flew home?"

"I flew home and I wasn't in the house ten minutes before the phone rang. It was Danny. I'd given him my home number and told him to call if he wanted to talk some more. I could sense that he needed to talk, so we just picked it up where we had left off early that morning and spent the next hour just getting to know each other a little better. I was painfully conscious of how little time he had left. That he wanted to spend any of it with me was both flattering and a little daunting. Anyway, we talked for about an hour, and we've been talking ever since. Three, four, five times a day, for a few minutes to a couple of hours."

"That's got to be a big hunk of your day," I said.

"It's a privilege. I had a long talk with Vic once. The doctor? Well, I've had lots of long talks with him, and with Celeste, too, but this was early on and he kind of quizzed me on how I was doing. He said he could wean Danny off me if it was becoming too much, but he had to do it sooner than later, because if he became attached to me and I abandoned him it would be disastrous. So speak now, was his message. I told him I was in till the end. I'd never abandon Danny. He said he knew that's what I'd say."

"Have you ever met the doctor?"

"Only on the phone, but we talk a lot. I count him among my few best friends. He's kind of become my doctor, too. I call him for minor complaints. For more serious stuff, I call him first, then run by him every procedure and prescription. He's saved me from a lot of discomfort."

"But you've never met him in person?"

"It feels like I have, but, no, not yet. I mean, I could, I guess, but he's with Danny all the time, except for the rare ride on his Harley."

"He has a Harley, too?"

"Yeah, we have that in common, but he's been riding a lot longer that I have. I started when I was fifty."

"That's a popular option, ain't?"

I got a smile out of him. "What else can you do when you hit fifty?" he said.

"I'll let you know." I wanted him to think I was younger. It embarrasses me to admit it. "Have you ever met the mother?"

"Yes, I have."

"Just on the telephone?"

"No, in person. HBO flew her down, just to meet everybody."

"Did HBO fly me down?"

"No, you come out of my Fox overhead. Why?"

"I thought you were footing that."

"No, I don't pay for anything. That's what overhead is all about."

"So who's paying my fee?"

"Ah. That one is mine. Some charges are best kept out of the overhead."

Whatever.

I asked him, "What was the mother like?"

"She's a saint. A beautiful, beautiful woman. For the past fifteen years she's been running a counseling and crisis center out of a Seattle storefront. The Sunrise Service Center. You know it?"

"Doesn't ring a bell."

"Celeste is a trained psychologist. She founded the center. She saw the need and just went and did it. It wrecked her first marriage, because she spent all her time making the center work. Now her energies go into making this little boy happy for whatever time he has left. She's disrupted her own life, moved out her own children, so she can tend to Danny. Totally devoted. I didn't know there were people like that."

"Why?" I asked. I thought it was a fair question.

"Why what?"

"Why has she devoted her life to this kid?"

"He's that kind of kid. Everybody who meets him is willing to go the distance for him. Her, the doctor, *me*. His agent, his publisher. Everybody who knows him. And a lot of people are getting to know him. Oprah wants him on her show. He's a wonder."

"And everybody who knows him knows him only on the phone?"

"*Only?* You can get to know a person really well on the phone. In Danny's case it's got to be that way. Except for his phone and his computer, his mom and Vic make up his whole world now."

"Oprah talks to him?"

"Yes, actually, now and then. He really likes her."

"Who doesn't? But what about his past friends, his teachers?"

"What about them?"

"Do they talk to him? Have they talked to you?"

"We'll get into that, but I don't want to get ahead of myself."

"He's in hiding, ain't?"

Krapp lowered his head, just short of a nod.

"Even though he's dying?" I asked. "Why is that?"

"We'll get into it. Later."

"What's the reluctance?"

He hesitated. He rolled a pen across his desk.

"I need to know you a little better."

"Me? What's to know, and why? I'm a snooper, for a fee."

But as I thought about it, I remembered shaking his hand, and how he seemed to be examining me.

"I've got to ease into this. Indulge me."

"You're the client and the meter's running, so whatever you say."

We sat in silence for a moment. It made me a little uncomfortable.

"You married?" I asked him.

"Yes, but my wife lives in Santa Barbara. Why do you ask?"

What I said was true but only half of why I asked: "I'm wondering if you're attracted to the mother."

"I love her, but not in that way. She's not my type."

"Oh, and what is your type?"

Sometimes I just can't help myself.

His discomfort held the words back, but finally he said, "She's morbidly obese."

"Say what?"

"Three hundred, three fifty, in that range. Maybe more; it's hard to guess those things."

"That's a big lady."

"Big lady, big heart."

"Doesn't much matter, you're married anyway."

"That's right."

"Happily?"

"Quinn, this isn't about my marriage."

"Knowing me, knowing you. Your wife lives in another city. Somebody would wonder about that."

"We have a platonic marriage. But I said I needed to know *you* a little better."

"Me, if I'd wanted a platonic marriage I would have married Plato."

He laughed, but he looked, if possible, a tad sadder.

"It wasn't always that way," he said.

"No, nothing ever is."

Now two of us were sad, prisoners of our own memories.

"Anyway, this isn't about me," he said.

"It's not about me, either. But for some reason you're avoiding what it *is* about."

9

I'D NEVER BEFORE SPENT SO MUCH TIME WITH A CLIENT TRY-
ing to find out just what it was he needed from me. With anyone else it would have been annoying. I admit, though, that
my interest was piqued. What did Alex Krapp need to know
about me before he could let it all hang out? Whatever, I
wanted to know more about the fat lady and her newly con-
stituted family and the kid who could remember being born.

Before he could go on, however, he got an urgent call
from a producer friend who was bringing him up to date on a
project and running a problem by him: The producer and his
partners had eighty-plus million invested into a star-driven fu-
turistic yarn that in rough cut made no sense. It had a beginning, middle, and end, but none of it hung together. Test
audiences didn't understand it. Editing was not going to save
them. The director, an A-list auteur, said he could solve the
lack of clarity by bringing back everybody to shoot just two
more scenes, but he had said that once before, when only sev-
enty million had been on the line, and it *still* didn't work.

They were not going to sink any more money into this. Krapp agreed they had a problem. He wondered aloud if they could salvage the movie with a stylish narration, a film noir kind of voice-over from the hero. The producer loved the idea but worried that the star would resist it. Well, yes, he probably will, said the screenwriter, but that's because it wasn't his idea, and it would require him to leave his chalet in Vail during prime ski time. Once he actually started doing it he would love it, Krapp predicted. The producer had known that Krapp would grasp immediately the difficult situation and come up with a fix. Could he do the narration in two weeks, in his spare time? What spare time? asked Krapp. The producer pleaded. Buy that Prius you have your eye on, make a statement. Krapp told him he had his eye on a new Mercedes, like the one Warner Brothers gave Richard Dreyfuss, and he saw it with a case of B.R.Cohn 1996 Olive Hill Estate Cabernet in the trunk.

Krapp ended the conversation and turned to me. "I hate to do this to you, but could you chill for a couple of hours? I have to go look at this rough cut. It's right on the lot so I shouldn't take too long."

"Sure, go ahead. Take your time. I'm on the clock."

"Anything you want, ask Gwendolyn. I'll be back as soon as I can."

He slipped the microrecorder into his jacket and left.

I called my office phone and checked messages. Apart from three offers to secure a low-cost mortgage at a favorable rate, I had zip.

I thought about calling some dudes I used to know on the LAPD, but they had to be retired by now. I was the baby of the precinct back then. We hadn't stayed in touch after I moved to Spokane with Connors.

When I'd first met Connors he liked it that I was a cop. It turned him on. Compared with his life behind the Rite Aid pharmacy counter, mine looked exciting. He liked to refer to me as his girlfriend the cop. Then when things got serious and he realized I spent my working day with dudes, some of them damn good-looking, and in some intense situations, he didn't like it quite so much. I fell out of touch with everybody.

There wasn't much of a view from Krapp's office window: part of the parking lot and part of what looked like a street in old New York.

The suction cup was still on his phone, the end of the wire dangling over the side of the desk. I should care. I've been known to hijack a phone conversation myself, so what? I told myself again: I'm not a cop anymore. I can go to a party where people are smoking grass, maybe even take a toke of my own. If I were invited. Which I'm mostly not. I can witness petty crimes and not feel duty-bound to make a bust. In fact, I was about to commit one. I slid open the desk drawer below the phone. It was filled with microcassettes, layered in tiers, hundreds of them, each labeled with a cataloguing code.

I quietly shut the drawer and went out to sit with Gwendolyn.

"Have you worked with him for long?" I asked her.

"About a year. His deal here is for two years."

"What then?"

"They either renew his deal or he moves on and I go back to the pool. I work mostly for writers who come unattached, without any assistants. It's all short-term, unless they're renewed, which most of them aren't, unless they come up with something good. Then they'll try to keep him here forever."

"It's a nice job?"

"Sure. Mostly just answering the phone and making reservations."

"I guess you get to meet a lot of interesting people, especially on the phone."

"Oh, sure, lots." She sat with her hands in her lap, waiting for the phone to ring. "What do you do," she asked, "up there in Seattle?"

I was glad Krapp hadn't told her.

"I'm a research consultant," I said, which wasn't that far from the truth.

"Oh. What are you working on with Alex?"

"Nautical law."

Don't ask me where that came from. When a lie is required, a lie magically appears.

She seemed satisfied with my presence. She took off her glasses and cleaned them. I noticed a one-inch scar starting at the corner of her right eye. Looked like she ran into something once.

"So when movie stars call," I said, "do you get to, you know, have a little conversation with them?"

"Who do you mean?"

"Nobody in particular. Just generally."

"Sometimes. Like Dustin Hoffman. He's always fun to talk to."

"What about Danny?"

"I love Danny! Do you know him?"

"Not personally."

"What a sweetheart. What a little doll. And what an inspiration. He's very sick, you know. My heart is going to break when he . . . you know."

"Have you met his mother? Celeste?"

"I've talked to her. She's a little distant with me. I'm just the secretary. But to Danny, everybody is special. He truly believes that. I try to believe that, too, though it's not always easy."

"What about Doctor Vic?"

"A real charmer. He sounds like a hoodlum, but that's just an act. Deep down he's all heart. I have some menopause issues and he's been a lot of help."

"Really? I have to talk to him. Any given moment, I'm likely to explode. Sometimes I have fire shooting out of my ears."

"Stay away from estrogen. That's what Vic says. Better to live with the hot flashes than roll the dice against cancer. His words. Do you use the ring?"

"No, I'm not married."

"Neither am I, but, you know, I'm ever hopeful. If I meet a guy I want to be ready. For him. I could care less."

"My motto."

"You play the hand you're dealt."

"What's worse, a woman having a husband who turns her off and she doesn't want, or a man having a wife who turns him on but he can't have?"

"Is that a trick question?"

"I'm not even sure it's a question."

"Anyway, Vic said to take the ring out. Just go cold turkey and hope the feelings will return and the hot flashes go away. You got to think of the future. It's not worth cancer down the line."

"Sounds like you've had some pretty intimate conversations with Vic."

"Well, he is a doctor."

"Have you ever recorded any of those conversations?"

"Lord, no, why would I do that?"

"People do."

"Well, I don't."

I changed the subject.

"She's a little cold, the mother, you said?"

"Danny and Alex adore her, so maybe it's just me."

"Does Vic adore her?"

"Funny, he never talks about her. I can't remember him ever using her name. He's sick, too, you know."

"Yeah, I heard. AIDS, right?"

"But he's not gay. He's bisexual."

"And that's not gay?"

"No, because that's a choice. He can choose one or the other. He kind of prefers men, but not exclusively."

"Wow, you have had some real conversations with that bunch."

"Well, when they call the office, I'm the first one they talk to."

"And how often do they call the office?"

"Every day—Danny, at least. A few times a day, when Alex is here. Why are you interested?"

"Only because Mr. Krapp has spent all morning telling me about Danny and the others, instead of what I'm here for."

"I'm not surprised. Danny has changed his life. And between you and me, he needed to change his life."

"How so?"

She whispered, "Depression. He was going downhill, kind of fading away, until Danny came into his life."

"And talking to a boy on the phone, that's helped it?"

"Like night and day. Have you read the script?"

"His adaptation? No, I wouldn't have any reason to read it."

"Too bad, because it's beautiful. I cried. It's a sure Emmy, you can take that to the bank. And it was written right in that office, at a high rate of speed, because Alex wanted Danny to be able to read the finished script. He faxed him pages every night of what he had written that day, and I can tell you he's never done that before with anyone. Not Dustin Hoffman, not anyone. No A-list writer ever does that. But he did it with that little boy. Showed him daily pages. I'd stay here with him, just to fax the pages. I'm union, so my day normally ends at six, but I'd stay till seven, eight o'clock. On the day he finished the last scene and I faxed it to Danny, we cracked open a bottle of champagne and sat around for an hour or so waiting for his response. We waited and waited, and finally Doctor Vic called and he sounded pissed, so I put him right through." Her voice dropped to a whisper. "I listened in."

"Your secret is safe with me."

"Vic said, 'What the hell did you say to Danny? He's crying. He won't talk to anybody.' Alex told him to put Danny on the line. I could hear Vic telling him it was Alex, but Danny didn't want to talk. Finally, though, he took the phone and while Vic and Celeste were in the room with him, he told Alex how moved he was by the screenplay, how it captured all that he wanted to say about his life, how it was beyond his most optimistic hopes, and how he could die happy now, knowing that because of Alex his true story could be told so well and reach millions of people, millions of kids. God, I cried myself. Afterward, Alex came out of the office and gave me a big hug, the only time he ever did that, and I swear he was crying, too. This is a tough guy in a tough business, I can tell you, but he was crying."

I didn't say anything. As far as I could see, nobody had a problem that fell under what I do for work. A small fifteen-year-old wasn't going to see sixteen. That was a problem nobody was going to fix.

10

THE IVY HAS BEEN THERE FOREVER. I CAN REMEMBER CRUIS-
ing it in the old black and white, trying to spot some movie
stars on the patio, back when I could actually finger movie
stars. Now, I can't tell one from another. I never had a call to
go to the Ivy in those days—nothing bad ever happened
there—and no way could I afford to eat there. I still can't afford to eat there, but eat there I did, arriving in Alex Krapp's
Porsche.

In my purse were about twenty microcassettes that I had
talked him into lending me. He was reluctant to do it, which
I could understand. I had no solid reason for wanting them
beyond a hunch that it might be useful for me to recognize the
voices of the players. I assured him that I would guard his cassettes with my life, which is easy enough to say when you
think you won't ever have to.

The valet knew both the writer and the Porsche.

Nobody dresses anymore, so I looked fine. I was the only
one who cared. Everybody gives you a quick scan when you

go into a place like that, but it only takes them a second to dismiss you as, if not a tourist, a person of no great consequence in their world. Nobody noticed Alex Krapp either, except for the maitre d', who said, *"Bonsoir, Monsieur Krapp. Ça va?"*

"Ça va," said my host. *"Et vous?"*

"Bien, merci."

"Pouvons-nous avoir une table sur le patio, s'il vous plaît?"

We followed the maitre d' to the patio. I looked at Alex Krapp and cocked an eye.

He smiled. "The benefits of a private liberal education."

It was nice to sit outside. I would not be eating alfresco in Seattle for a couple more months, and then at some place not so charming. We ordered Sapphire Blue Martinis.

Forest Whitaker left his wife with another couple to come over to say hello to Krapp. Alex had some years before written a small picture in which Whitaker played the lead. He congratulated the actor on his recent Oscar nomination and assured him he was a lock.

We toasted his chances.

Krapp had already apologized for leaving me all afternoon while he was involved in trying to salvage an eighty-million-dollar investment, but he made amends again. We drank to eighty million dollars, and toasted once more, this time to the purity of art.

"I hated to wake you up," he said.

"I'd still be asleep if you hadn't."

I'd been fast asleep on his davy when he came back to the office.

"It's that sofa. I often take a long nap there myself."

I knew that. I'd felt the imprint of his body.

I ordered the crab cakes and, on his recommendation, the grilled vegetables, which proved to be a good choice. Instead of a second round of martinis, he ordered a bottle of chardonnay, the very same wine that shot out of my nose when he told me that Alex Krapp was not his real name.

I asked him what his real name was, but he wouldn't tell me.

"Although I suppose that you could find it. You are a detective, after all."

I was having such a good time I'd forgotten. It was almost like a date, if I could remember what a date was like.

"One thing," I said. "How does a fifteen-year-old boy even get a book published? Did he just send it to a publisher or an agent?"

"Nobody gets a book published that way. That would be like sending a screenplay to a studio or to the William Morris building. Nobody there would have enough information to form an opinion."

"What information?"

"Like, is the thing any good?"

"Isn't that what they're supposed to know?"

"Collectively. Nobody knows anything on his own."

"Then how did Danny sell his book?"

"The kid's a voracious reader. After he got home from the hospital he was pretty much confined to his bed, so he read everything in the house. His new mother, Celeste, was a reader herself so she had a lot on her shelves. One of those books was a memoir by a well-known author dying of AIDS. Owen Robbe. You know him?"

I read a little myself, but him I didn't know, which didn't mean he wasn't famous.

"He's pretty good. Was. He's dead now. He was one of gay literature's shining lights."

"There's a gay literature?"

"Yes, and it's a good market. Twenty, twenty-five percent of the population is gay, and they read in greater numbers than the straight population. Vic told me that one of the shrinks Danny talks to—"

"He talks to shrinks?"

"Star shrinks, like Doctor Phil, Joyce Brothers, people like that. They love him. They hear about the book, read it, and get in touch with him, and since he can't refuse anybody he talks to them. Anyway, one of them said to Celeste, 'You know Danny is gay, don't you?' "

"Is he?"

"No way. Who cares, anyway? He's dying. That's all that we care about. The kid is in a state of arrested development, physically. He's fifteen and hasn't passed through puberty yet, because of all the medication he takes and all the physical abuse he's been through. But from the talks I've had with him I'm almost a hundred percent sure he's straight. The gays think he must be gay because nobody straight could be that sensitive."

"Gays are sensitive?"

We had a little laugh and tried to remember the point. Danny had read this book by Owen Robbe.

"The book made a deep impression on him. They were kindred spirits. Danny located the author's Web site and sent him an e-mail telling him how much he loved the book and how much it helped him, because he had AIDS, too, with all the complications, and he knew he was terminal. He had talked it over with his mother and he was working on coming to terms with it. Robbe's book helped, he said. Danny figured the guy got thousands of e-mails and didn't expect to hear anything back, but Robbe got back to him. It was your basic 'glad you enjoyed it' kind of reply, but he wondered how a young boy even came upon his book, which was not meant for youngsters. Danny told him a little lie, something to make the encounter more interesting than just saying he got it from his mom. He told him that on one of his trips to the hospital he traded off some sports magazines for the book; I think he wanted to sound macho. Well, it amused Robbe and an e-mail correspondence began. After a short time Robbe gave Danny his phone number and they started to talk. Danny told him about the things that had happened to him and what he tried to do to overcome the horrors of his life. Robbe encouraged him to write down all those stories; if nothing else, it would be a catharsis. As the stories came in, Robbe read them and was very moved. He urged the kid to keep going, make a book out of it. When Danny finished the book, Robbe sent it to his agent, who loved it and signed Danny on. She sent it to Robbe's publisher, to his own editor, who also loved it and started a phone relationship with Danny himself. He's been his champion at the publishing house."

"It must have been a blow to the kid when his mentor died."

"He was devastated. It felt like another abandonment. He dedicated the book to Robbe and it became a good seller, a best seller in a few smaller markets, and of course there was the deal with HBO, which can boost the book sales, big-time. Nobody who has read it doesn't like it. You can't *not* like it."

"Well, yeah, he's fifteen and dying."

"True, there is no way to separate that from the story. *That* is what the book is about. But it transcends that."

"How much did Owen Robbe help him with it?"

"Ah, that is a troublesome question. Danny claims not at all, beyond his encouragement to keep on writing, and I believe him, but a few critics have suggested that Robbe actually wrote the book."

"Would that be a crime?"

"Good question, but it's moot. The man is dead. He said he didn't write it. Nothing he left behind indicated he wrote the stories, none of his friends can claim that he did, and both Danny and his mother insist he didn't."

I'd begun to call him Alex. He'd ordered a second bottle of wine and I was feeling chummy.

"Alex, we've spent practically the whole day together, and it's been a pleasant break for me, but you've got to tell me what it is you want me to do."

He took a deep breath and another sip of wine.

"Have you ever heard of a reporter named Eve Gosler?" he asked me.

"TV type? I don't watch TV."

"No, magazines, the big glossy kind."

"I read them at the hairdresser's."

"Well, then, you know *Vanity Fair*."

"Sure. Thick thing. I look at the ads."

"It has a wide circulation."

"I'm sure. So Eve Gosler reports for *Vanity Fair*?"

"Yes. She's an investigative reporter and she's working on a long story. The story, well . . ."

When he hesitated, I said, "Is she trying to prove that Owen Robbe wrote Danny's book?"

"No, she's trying to prove that Danny doesn't even exist."

11

ALEX DROVE ME TO THE AIRPORT. I WAS A LITTLE WORRIED about getting there in one piece, but the screenwriter held his booze much better than I, and that sleek Porsche seemed supernaturally connected to the road.

Given the lag time for *Vanity Fair,* the story this reporter, Eve Gosler, was doing on Danny was still, at best, a couple of months away from publication. HBO, though, was not waiting until then to get nervous. They informed Alex that they were not going to go ahead with the project unless they could verify the author's existence.

It's fairly easy to prove that someone walks the earth, but it's impossible to prove that someone does not. Thus, the power of priests.

HBO put it all on the screenwriter. It was up to him to prove that the boy he'd been talking to for hours each day, for a whole year, the one who called him Poppa, was real. I heard the kid myself on the speakerphone. He sounded real enough to me. But if you can't see it, is it?

"Everyone she's interviewed, including me," said Krapp, "has tried to convince her that Danny is real. His editor and publisher and agent and so many others, we've all begged her not to do the story. One of the weapons used against little Danny, while he was still in his father's clutches, was the assurance that no one would ever believe him. It's every pedophile's strongest weapon. Don't tell. If you do, nobody will believe you."

The sad-eyed screenwriter took the ramp onto the Santa Monica Freeway and the centripetal force sucked me toward him, a not altogether unpleasant feeling. After we got on the straightaway and were going a smooth and easy eighty miles per hour, I said, "It looks like an easy fix to me. You arrange a meet in Danny's home. . . . You know where he lives, don't you?"

"Not exactly."

"What does that mean?"

"I send mail, little gifts and things, to Celeste at her service center."

"Is there any reason why they don't want you to know where they live?"

"It's not just me. Anybody. For one thing, all his admirers would beat a path to his door."

Okay, that was one thing, but I could sense it wasn't the real thing.

"Whatever. They make an exception for you. To save the movie and get out his message . . . and I'm guessing there's a payment due if the movies goes."

"Over a hundred thousand, and they could use the money. I've offered to give Celeste money, for medical bills and all that, but she's always refused it. She says they're fully covered under her husband's GI insurance."

"And he's in Iraq, right?"

"Yes. Apparently in some sensitive assignment. He can't say exactly where he is, but they do get e-mails from him. Danny really misses him."

"Okay, so here's what you do: You go to the house, you suit up, do whatever the other two have to do to tend to him, and you spend one minute in his presence. You take a picture of the two of you together and you report back to HBO and the show goes on."

"I've been pleading with Celeste to let me do just that, ever since HBO gave me the ultimatum. That's when I found out that Danny and his adopted family have more to worry about than the diseases ravaging him."

"I can't imagine what could be worse."

I was learning that with Alex everything takes a minute or two.

"This reporter isn't budging," he said, "until she has some hard evidence, and the problem is she can't find anything—no school records or arrest records on Danny's father, or anything else that usually establishes a person's story. Obviously, that looks suspicious, unless you know."

"Know what?"

"Danny's real last name is a well-kept secret, even to me, his Poppa, and I wouldn't be shocked to learn that his first name was changed as well. They're doing everything they can to seal any paper trail, with the help of city and state officials, who were prevailed upon to bend the rules in Danny's case."

"Why? What's so special about his case? And why can't you or anyone else find a way to visit Danny?"

"For my own safety," Alex told me.

"Yes, but if you take all the precautions . . ."

"It's not the medical thing. Yes, he's very sick and susceptible to everything, but the danger to me comes from another source."

Damned if I was going to ask what. But this time I didn't have to wait longer than it took for him to take a breath and say, "His birth parents were part of a Satanic cult. A powerful and particularly vicious cult."

I hear the word *cult*, Satanic or otherwise, and my eyes glaze over. Basically, cults are just another way for perverts to get what they want sexually, which is reason enough to worry about your children falling into one, but I don't get all hysterical when I find out that a charismatic lunatic and a dozen dingbats have taken up residence in the Olympic Mountains. When I was a cop in Spokane we'd get a little spillover from Idaho, where if you're to believe the rumors, cults abound, everything from the KKK and the Aryan Brotherhood to polygamists and cattle mutilators. I used to put it all under the heading of: GET A LIFE! That was then.

"Remember I told you about Randy Merck?" I said.

"Yes."

"One of the neighbors told me that the family was part of a Satanic cult."

"I didn't want to say anything at the time, but when you told me about the similarities I knew it wasn't a coincidence. Satanists all have common practices and rituals."

"Over all those years?"

"Over generations. They're out there, all over, in every walk of life: teachers, lawyers, clergy, politicians, cops . . ."

"But why should Celeste be afraid for Danny? I mean, he's terminal, and at least for the time he has left, he's safe with her and Vic, ain't?"

"Danny was a special boy, even in that environment, *especially* in that subculture. Apart from the fact that he knows too many names and has seen too many things, he embodies everything the Satanists despise most. Innocence. No matter what they did to him, they could never defile him. They would have killed him long ago, while he was still under their control, but they wanted to break him more than they wanted to sacrifice him. They wanted to befoul him. They wanted to possess his soul. But that sick little boy wouldn't let them. He took every horrible abuse they could give him, and he never gave in to them. He clung to the innocence and the love that was in his heart. Finally, his attempt at suicide was in defiance of them. They would never break him."

"But Danny's parents are out of the picture now, ain't?"

"One of them is," said Alex Krapp.

"And the mother is on the arfy-darfy, ain't?"

"If that means on the lam, yes. She's a fugitive. Maybe. Or maybe she's dead, murdered by the cult. Or maybe she's alive and she's a great danger to Danny and anyone near him."

"Who thinks she's alive and dangerous?"

"Danny. He knows she's dangerous, and he knows she held a high position in the cult. She wasn't just a follower. Some of these people are very important and well-placed. They don't want to wait for Danny to die. These are insane, vicious, and very clever people. Now you know why I had to take my time with you."

"The hell I do."

"I had to be comfortable you weren't one of them."

Insulting, yes, but under the circumstances, I let it slide.

"I like to say I'm fearless, which I'm not," I said, "but I can't work up the heebie-jeebies over some batty Satanists. Okay. So I've got to look over my shoulder for devil worshippers while I prove once and for all that Danny exists. Is that it? Is that the job?"

"That's the job."

"All right. It's on."

"How will you do it?"

"I don't know."

"You don't know?"

"One thing will lead to another. It always does."

"Look, Danny exists. Eventually Eve Gosler will verify that. But HBO won't wait. I can't have this project go away. I need you to verify Danny's existence, but you can never, ever, let Danny, or anyone else, know that I hired you. This is very delicate. It would kill Danny if he thought I doubted him. Hiring you would be seen by him as a betrayal."

"I'll do my best."

"No, you *have* to keep this secret. If I lose Danny, I lose the HBO project."

"It's not about any movie project, we both understand that."

He fell silent.

We were heading up Airport Boulevard, toward the airport, when he made a right toward long-term parking.

"Where're you going?"

"I'm going to park the car."

"Here? Why?"

"I'm going up to Seattle with you."

In my boozy uncertainty I heard it as some kind of romantic gesture, like a city man seeing an island date to the ferry and then impulsively jumping onto the boat with her. Aw-w-w-w-w. I'd drunk the minimum required to render me goofy.

"You're going to fly to Seattle? Now? Just as you are?"

"I do it often. I have a house up on Bainbridge Island. You see, I'm one of those people who do need an island."

"Then why the hell did I fly down here?"

"I didn't know I'd be going back, and I wanted to start on this right away. Are you upset with me?"

"No, I've had a nice day."

"Good, I'm glad."

"And you have a house down here, in LA?"

"Not anymore. I have a suite at the Sofitel, across from the Beverly Center. The price is reasonable and when I get off the elevator I smell Paris. I think it's the furniture polish they use."

"And your wife lives in Santa Barbara?"

"Yes."

"Why?" Sometimes I get personal. I can't help it.

"Women seem to like me . . ." he said, and paused. I knew this one did. "A few of them have loved me, but apparently there's some kind of price to pay for that. I don't really understand it."

"So you're separated."

"No, not legally."

"Just physically and emotionally?"

I kind of wished.

"Physically, yes, obviously. Emotionally, we're still very much involved."

"Movie people live different, ain't?"

"It has nothing to do with movies."

"Does she know Danny, your wife?"

"Sure. He still calls her once in a while. Vic and Celeste, too. I think she kind of has a crush on Vic. He's a very engaging guy."

"Does she come up to the island?"

"During the summer, for a few weeks. She can't stand it this time of year."

He parked the car and we took the shuttle. Since it was a late flight, first class was available. He bought a ticket, we got on board, and this is where you came in, ain't? Me in the airplane can, trying to keep from exploding, feeling twinges I haven't felt in years, wondering what the hell.

Krapp's Cassette #DT-2 (partial)

—Mr. Krapp, it's Danny Timpkins.

—Hi, Danny, how're you doing?

—Pretty good, today. Did you have a nice flight back from
New York?

—It was all right.

—I enjoyed our talk last night.

—I did too. Are you usually up that late?

—Yeah. The fevers spike at night. It really helped to have
somebody to talk to, somebody besides Mom and Vic.

—Anytime. It'll be my pleasure.

—Really?

—Sure.

—You wouldn't mind—talking to me?

—No way. I'd love to talk to you.

—You gave me your home number but I didn't know if it
would be all right to call you there.

—It's fine. You can call me here or at my office. You call
whenever you want to. We can just shoot the shit.

(*Danny giggles*)

—*I'd really like that. I don't let too many people get close to me, because . . . Well, I just don't. But I felt like a real connection was made, you and me. After I talked to you last night I went right to sleep. I slept till noon.* (*Giggles*) *Then I was hungry so Mom went out and got me a pizza. It was the first time I had an appetite in a while.*

—*What do you like on your pizza?*

—*Olives and peppers. How about you?*

—*Pepperoni and anchovies.*

—*Really?*

—*Yeah, my favorite, what can I say?*

—*I don't eat meat or fish. I snack on fruit and I like pasta. My mom makes great pasta. And eggplant lasagna, I like that.*

—*Have you always been a vegetarian?*

—*Well . . . I always wanted to be, but . . .*

—*But?*

—*Sometimes they would force me to eat a steak with them.*

—*Your parents?*

—*Yeah. They liked steaks, rare, but they would put a raw one on my plate, dripping blood, and they would make me eat it until I'd have to run and throw up. They thought it was funny.*

—*Danny, that's horrible.*

—*You don't have to put that in the screenplay, do you?*

—*Not if you don't want me to.*

—*I'd rather it be about the good stuff. There was some good stuff. School 'n stuff.*

—*You know, though, that we'll have to deal with some of the bad things that happened to you.*

—*I know. I trust you. You write it the way you see it. I'm*

just hoping I'll be around to read it. I know I'll never see
it on TV. *(Silence)* Mr. Krapp?
—You can call me Alex.
—You all right? I'm sorry I brought up that stuff about raw
meat, but . . .
—Don't censor yourself when you talk to me, Danny.
Okay?
—Okay.
—I'm excited to start the screenplay.
—Mom said it could win an Emmy. Brad, my editor, said so,
too.
—Who knows? We won't think about that now, though.
We'll just think about writing the best screenplay we can.
—I love it when you say we. It makes me feel like, I don't
know, like you got my back.
—That's the right feeling.

12

I STOOD IN LINE AT THE STARBUCKS IN MY BUILDING, ON THE ground floor. Through the window I could see my three Indians, still sleeping under the pergola.

Cash, the barista kid, saw me over the top of his workstation and said, "Morning, Quinn. Double-tall nonfat?"

"Morning, Cash. Thank you."

"We're promoting the next big thing today—cinnamon dolce. Wanna live dangerously?"

"Hell, no."

"C'mon, Quinn, take it for a test drive. People are crazy mad for it."

"I won't like it."

"You don't like it, tomorrow's is free."

"Deal."

I took the drink across the street and up to my office. I sat behind my desk and popped the top and tried the latest concoction. I've heard that everyone is born with a preference for either sugar or salt. I must be one of the salty ones. The cinnamon dolce made my teeth hiss. On the upside, it was free. I took another sip.

I flipped through two phone books looking for the Sunrise Service Center. I called Information, but they didn't have a listing. I called the screenwriter's office.

Gwendolyn's cheery voice: "Good morning, Alex Krapp's office."

"Hey, Gwendolyn, it's Quinn."

" 'Morning, Quinn. He isn't here. He's not coming in today."

"Yeah, I know. I figured you'd have the address for the Sunrise Service Center? The place Krapp sends some stuff to?"

"Oh, sure, I do all the shipping and mailing."

"Could I have it?"

"Why would you want that?"

Oops. I was supposed to be a consultant on marine law. I came up with something quick.

"I wanted to send Danny a little gift and a card. After talking to Alex all of yesterday I feel I know the kid."

"That's sweet. He'll like that. You got a pen?"

I wrote down the address and approached my latte on its blind side. I leaned back and sipped the sickly sweet concoction.

Some screenwriter. He bought an island house. For a boy he's never seen. He thought that if he had a house close by, Danny could come and stay with him someday. He could take him out in his boat and catch a salmon. He could bundle the kid in a blanket and they could sit on the deck and watch the sunset, all the things he never got to do with his own kids.

"Any chance of that?" I asked him, that night in the limo.

"There's always a chance, otherwise why even try? Just because they say he's going to die . . . Miracles happen."

"We put a man on the moon. Once."

"I have to hope."

"Do they know you have a house so close, on Bainbridge? Danny and the other two?"

"No. I want it to be a surprise, for when he gets well enough."

When he dropped me off, I said this stupid thing: "Would you like to come up?"

Da frick.

I hadn't said those words since I was, what, twenty-two?

I was a little lost in this notion that I was on a great date: flown first class to LA and back, wined and dined, introduced to a couple of movie stars. I should at least come across.

In the morning, my lack of professionalism stung me, but that night the alcohol buzz I was in cushioned me.

"I wouldn't want to miss the last ferry," he said.

How cool would that be, if he missed the ferry and sort of had to stay the night.

"It's only a three-minute walk from here," I told him.

He lowered his head and looked up at my building through the limo window, as though looking for possible escape routes. I do that myself, with other people's buildings.

"My office is just a diagonal from here, across the square, in the Pioneer Building." I told him. "I have a short commute."

What was the subtext? I can stay in bed a little longer than the average tramp?

He sent the driver on his way and we rode up the elevator to the eighth floor.

Once I had a boy put the moves on me in a rising elevator, also back when I was about twenty-two. I liked it a lot. Especially knowing that the door would save me if I stopped liking it.

Alex Krapp, a gentleman and a grown-up, stood with his back against the opposite wall, I with my hands digging for my keys.

I opened the door to my apartment, took his coat, and offered him a cup of coffee.

"No, thanks, it would keep me awake all night."

"Me too."

Not that there's anything wrong with that. I'm often up all night anyway, and without such pleasant company.

"Nice place," he said.

"It's somebody's condo, an investment somebody made. I have a year's lease."

Then I said stupid thing, part two: "No one's ever been here. Besides me, I mean."

"Get out."

"It just worked out that way."

"No one? Ever?"

"Oh, God. I forgot. There was someone. He's dead now."

"I'm a little afraid of you right now."

I laughed, and thank God, so did he.

"I wish I could show you something and say, 'That was my grandmother's.' But I never had that kind of life."

I offered him tea, a drink, a blow job. (I'm just being silly now. Maybe I should have been *then*, too.)

"No, thanks." (He might have said that to the other offer, too, and I would have been crushed.)

He went to the window and took in the view. My Indians

were back on their post. I stood next to him, our arms touching, and showed him my office window across the square. We moved to one edge of the window where we could see a sliver of Puget Sound. I pointed out how far up First Avenue we could see.

"It's nice up here," he said.

It felt a little like one, but, let's face it, it wasn't a real date. It lacked the basics: two people exploring the romantic possibilities. Here we had one person trying to remember what it was like—me—and another wondering what he was doing in his new detective's apartment. The screenwriter. Maybe there would be something he could use in a script someday.

I'm going to say, though I may be wrong, that we were brought to that awkward moment by my having taken Danny's case for granted, and by letting myself become distracted by the last thing I wanted, a man, something I was sure would never share what was left of my life.

Knowing that, it should have been simple, ain't? Suffer myself.

He was handsome in his own way, in a weathered way; physically fit, for a man his age; surprisingly sensitive for a Hollywood denizen; rich. As men go, this one was the gold standard. The best to be said for me, on the other hand, was that I cleaned up pretty good.

As I recall, we never did sit down. We talked as we moved from one window to another, together or crossing by each other, like the mating dance of some kind of dying species.

He told me about making his living for three years with a handmade seventeen-ounce cue stick and some fine English on the ball, before suiting up for Vietnam. He came out of that whole to the eye but missing something you can't weigh. He found it again taking writing courses at Cal State LA, and later as a reporter for the now defunct *LA Examiner.*

During a celebrity interview with a famously coked-out director, he stumbled upon a portal into Hollywood. Off the record, the director was bemoaning his difficulties in getting the script right for *How Mars Was Won,* a tent-pole event long promised but still undeliverable.

Alex Krapp, or whatever he was called then, listened to the director struggle to explain what wasn't working in his script. But that's not the problem, Alex told him. All that was wrong with the story was that some people were with the wrong people, just like what's wrong most of the time down here on Earth.

It was a major breakthrough.

"He hired me on the spot," Alex said, "at ten thousand a week, and this was in the seventies. It was more money than I'd ever seen before. After that, I worked on every picture he did, right up until that night he washed up on Latigo Beach."

On my kitchen counter I have a small replica of the Public Market clock. He caught sight of it and realized he had to leave if he were to catch that last ferry.

I would have liked him to stay, but.

At the door, we shook hands.

I think I had a mini-orgasm.

The next time I would see him would be because of a dead woman found in the new sculpture park.

13

I HAD A SLIGHT HANGOVER, HAVING WON THE DRINKING woman's trifecta the night before: hard liquor and wine at the Ivy, and a couple of beers on the plane ride home. Could I be getting too old for this kind of thing? If you have to ask . . .

I'd slept badly after Krapp left my place. After a long cool shower, I creamed my face and lay awake remembering how Connors used to sleep with his hands behind his head. A way of opening up his chest. He suffered sleep apnea, and I suffered along with him. Often, I would wake up to find him not breathing, a deadly stillness in the air. I'd look at him, scared stiff that he was dead, unable to touch him for fear he'd gone cold. Then, in a small burst, the air would puff out of his mouth and he would breathe again. Until the next episode, which could come in a minute or two. I wondered how Esther was dealing with that. Suffer, bitch.

Then I wondered how Alex slept, and with whom, and why I even wanted to know. I didn't want a man in my life unless he was cutting me checks, and for no longer than that took. Especially not a man waiting for a terminally ill boy to get better.

I finally dropped off, only to be awakened by my three Indians, who had once again started their tribal chant. It was too much. I went to the window and shouted down to the pergola. "Yo! Hey, David! Clifford!" One of these days I was going to have to get the third yonko's name. David, the skinny one, the lead singer, looked up. "Yo, Quinn! Where's yer fuckin' limo?"

"He didn't pick you up? I told him to pick you up, take you wherever you wanted to go."

The doofus actually looked around for the stretch.

"In your dreams," I yelled down. "Listen, no singing tonight, okay? And I mean all night. I'm dead up here."

They earnestly promised to keep it quiet. They were nothing if not earnest. But I couldn't get back to sleep anyway. I thought about Satanists. The only image I could conjure up was the face of Randy Merck's father, when I interviewed him in the prison on McNeil Island. I'd have to say he looked like hell.

A former neighbor had told me Merck was a Satanist, but I wouldn't want to hang a man on that testimony. Still, the yonko sent a chill down my spine. After talking to him I wanted to puke.

I wondered, though, about them. Are they any harder to handle than Muslim or Christian or Jewish fundamentalists? When it comes to a body count, the Satanists are rank amateurs compared with other true believers. Compared with a Taliban, the devil has class.

The fear Satanists engender is not so much in what we

know about them, but in what we don't know about them. Hell, I'm scared of the Masons. I don't know any more about them than I do about Satanists.

Nobody wants anybody lurking about in secret, is the thing. Especially PIs. If anybody is doing any lurking, the PI wants it to be him, and when I say him I mean me.

Why would Satanists be after a dying boy anyway, or his adoptive mother? Or some screenwriter who'd grown close to him? If the kid were going to reveal some deep dark secrets threatening to the cult, he would have already done it. Maybe he had and all they wanted now was revenge and to set an example for others. Forget about devil worshippers, I told myself, trying to get to sleep. I wonder if some of them are in Congress, I thought, and then slapped myself mentally; I'd never get to sleep at this rate. The hell with it. Let the Satanists knock themselves out. Two or three days, I'll find this kid, take a picture, maybe have a farewell dinner with Alex, and be on to the next thing.

BERNARD CAME INTO THE OFFICE AS I WAS LEAVING.

"Quinn, it's your lucky day, girl."

Bernard is a former LA Crip, street name Romeo. He took it on the arfy-darfy, from both the LAPD and his former colleagues, and settled into a more or less respectable life as a ticket scalper in Seattle. He has an office in the building. What he considers a stroke of luck never matches my own idea.

"I got one single for the Sonics game tonight."

He walked with me to the elevator.

"Fold it two ways and put it where the moon don't shine," I said.

It's not that I have zero interest in professional sports. I'll occasionally watch a game on TV, for as long as it takes me to quaff a Stella Artois at the Belltown Bistro. But I can't muster much civic pride for the hometown teams. The players would much rather be in LA or New York, the big markets. Bernard, though, has transferred his allegiances and is now a Seahawks-Mariners-Sonics booster and seldom is seen without some article of clothing affirming his support. Of course, adoration of the local teams is his bread and butter.

"I thought to myself," said Bernard, "who goes alone? Quinn! C'mon, girl, this seat's close enough you get hit by the sweat."

"Don't talk to me about sweat. I'm an expert."

"You don't even like *basketball*." His voice had a quality of plaintive disbelief.

"I used to, back when the Blue Devils played Ashland and I'd ride home from the game in the back of a Chevy with the center's arm around my shoulders."

"Relive those days! Recapture your youth."

"Listen to you, you're losing all street, Romeo."

He rode down the elevator with me, trying to save me from a lost opportunity of epic proportions. In the lobby he latched onto another tenant we knew, Mahlon, the theoretical architect, who basically designs castles in the sky. Bernard rode back up with him, trying to unload his last single ticket. Suffer.

I went across the street to my apartment parking garage and picked up the PT Cruiser. Aboveground and out of the alley, I pulled to the curb on Washington Street and punched the address for Sunrise Service Center into my Magellan.

The cool female voice on the Magellan sent me down Second Avenue where it runs into Fourth, then she told me to hang a left on Holgate and go up the incline to Beacon Hill. In a few more minutes she intoned, rather pleased with herself, "You have reached your destination, on the right."

The address was just off Beacon Way, on a diagonal slice, where most of the store signs were in Chinese, when they weren't in Spanish. I was looking for a storefront counseling and help center, but what I found instead was your basic mail drop. So soon on the case to discover that, as a politician might say, untruths have been disseminated. Why was I not surprised? If nobody ever lied I'd be out of business.

I pulled to the curb across the street from the mail drop. I could have gone inside but I knew that I would bump up against a confidentiality policy. Even if a twenty could overcome the policy, as often it can, I would be calling attention to myself. I didn't want anyone to tell Celeste that someone was snooping around. I would have blown Alex's only caution to me.

I called my new client. He sounded not unhappy to hear from me.

"Found anything yet?" he asked.

I told him it was a little early. "How's island life?"

"Transforming. Calming. I don't know why I just don't stay here. I'm so sick of LA. Maybe by this summer . . . you could come over. I'll barbecue a salmon."

Hello? That sounded like an invitation.

"Sure," I said, "but for right now, I'd like you to do something for me."

"What's that?"

"I want you to call up Celeste . . ."

"I was just talking to her. Danny called me and then she got on the phone."

"Oh, what did you talk about?"

"The problem. How we can get the movie going, short of putting Danny on a stage."

I didn't remind him that no one would want to drag the kid out of his bed and put him on a stage. Mostly likely, he was quoting the mother.

"Any ideas?" I asked.

"One. A pretty good one, actually. I have to run it by HBO and see if they'll buy it. She said she did some work in the past for the governor of Washington, whatshername?"

"Christine Gregoire."

"Right. Celeste did some work for her, some studies on child welfare, when Gregoire was lieutenant governor. They had a pretty good relationship. Gregoire was the one who made it possible to seal Danny's records, including all the records of his father's arrest and imprisonment."

"Why would she do that?"

"She recognized the danger to Danny. She knew one or two of those people, in political circles."

"Satanists?"

He didn't answer my question.

"And she was grateful to Celeste for all of her work, which was volunteered."

"So how does the gov figure in now?"

"Celeste is proposing to get the governor to vouch for Danny's existence. I think HBO would be good with that."

"So am I out of a job?"

"Not yet. But I kind of hope you will be."

"Because I'm already seeing something hinky."

"You are? What?"

He sounded crestfallen.

"I'd rather not say—not right now, anyway. It'll take that long for HBO to make up their mind, ain't?"

"They have a legal department. You know what it's like to have a legal department?"

"I don't even have a secretary."

"Having a legal department keeps you from ever having to make a decision. You said you wanted me to call Celeste?"

"Right. I want you to call her and say you forgot to send her something, or you have to send her something important, overnight. And then you send her something. No, you have Gwendolyn send her something, from LA."

"Send her what?"

"Anything. A book you got for Danny. An old movie script. Anything, but it's important that she get it tomorrow. Tell her you're sending it and she should look for it tomorrow. Okay?"

"I guess so. I feel funny about it."

"Snooping will do that, make you feel funny."

"If Danny finds out, it'll be a major crisis."

"I'll keep low."

14

I DROVE BACK TO THE PARKING GARAGE AND WALKED UP THE ramp. The alley had had a chance to ventilate since morning, but the cold city air still held that certain whiff of eau de piss. My three Indians were sprawled on the bench under the pergola, next to which someone had constructed two less than permanent monuments. Painted flat boards, side by side:

Chief	Far
Seattle	Away
Now	Brothers
The	And
Streets	Sisters
Are	We Still
Our	Remember
Home	You

The one on the left was decorated with dollar signs and crosses, the one on the right with abstract birds.

I took a quick detour to the Korean store and bought a liter of Pepsi, three ham and cheese sandwiches, and a carton of Marlboros. I dropped the grocery bag on their bench.

Alcoholics are basically sugar freaks, so they fell on the Pepsi almost as fast as they would have on booze. They cracked open the carton of smokes and lit up.

"You're all right, Quinn," said David, exhaling. "Not much to look at, but nice 'n loose with a buck." His tribal name is Hidesbehindthesmoke. Really.

I went up to the office.

The crisis hotline was invented in Seattle. They made a movie about it, *The Slender Thread,* starring Sidney Poitier, who in his prime could have had me with, "You wanna?" I think I might well have. And in my prime, who knows, he might have wanted me.

The city has always had a high rate of suicide, and there has been an ongoing debate over why that is. Duh? From November to March the sun neither rises and shines nor glows and sets. All that happens is the black becomes gray around nine in the morning and then turns black again around three-thirty, four in the afternoon. August, September, and October are gifts from heaven. Everybody tries to hold on until then, the number for the crisis line on a Post-it on the reefer. Some, too many, either lose the number or are too cranky to call. When that happens, well, up here it's legal to pack a gun and almost everybody does.

The rest of us just hope they don't take any innocent by-standers out with them. For the unlicensed, there are bridges within walking distance or a short bus ride away, there are overpasses, and there is the cold, deep, and unforgiving water surrounding the place. That was the out little Danny went for, stopped only by the fortuitous presence of a crisis hotline poster.

I punched out a number.

This is why *my* tribal name should be Quinn Runs-aroundincircles, should I ever find a tribe that would have me. When I don't know what else to do, I do something.

"Teen Crisis Line."

"Hello. Is Celeste there?" I put on my best teenage girl voice.

"My name is Mary. What's yours?"

"Once before I talked to Celeste. Can I talk to her again?"

"Gee, I don't know any Celeste, honey, but I can try to find her. Right now, though, let's you and I talk."

"I'll call back later."

"Wait . . ."

I called another number.

A man answered; I told him I dialed a wrong number.

I kept trying numbers and then, I swear, I got this: "Bingo hotline, what is your location?"

"Huh? What?"

"You want to locate a bingo game? Tell me where you are."

"Not playing bingo, lady."

It was late in the morning, and I was about ready to sprint up to Salumi's for one of Gina's killer porchetta and Gorgonzola sandwiches when I heard this soft comforting voice say, "Yes, I'm Celeste. When did I talk to you, honey?"

"I don't know, I was kinda high at the time, but you helped me."

I was back on my spacey teenager voice.

"Well, I'm glad I did. What's going on with you now?"

"I think I'm gonna jump off the Ballard Bridge."

"What would make you want to do something like that?"

"I had a friend did it. I guess he did it. I never heard from him again or saw him again, and he told me, 'cause of his father and mother doin' stuff to him, and being Satanists and everything, that he couldn't take it anymore and was gonna jump off something."

"Your friend wasn't making good choices. He should have called someone, like you have now. Let's talk about you."

"His name was Danny. My friend."

"Is it because of your friend that you're having these thoughts now?"

My luck, I got another volunteer with the same name.

"Maybe I talked to a different Celeste. This one worked with a dude named Bob. I think they're married or something."

"Hmmm, I don't know them. There are a couple Bobs around. But it sounds to me like you have more immediate things to deal with."

I talked to her for a minute or two more, long enough to tell her I was feeling much more positive now and I would go home and try to work things out. I casually asked again if there was another Celeste answering the phones. She said there might be, they had lots of volunteers, some of whom come and go.

I thanked her and assured her she wouldn't be hearing from me again. I would make good choices from now on. I wish.

I thought a bit about calling Randy Merck at Walla Walla. I could get him, no problem. The warden and I were tight, ever since we both watched a fat man hang and brooded together over the whole sad process. But a call like that shouldn't be made on an empty stomach, and maybe not on a full one, either. Investigating Randy had brought me close to hurling a couple times.

I ran up to Salumi's while I still had a gaping appetite.

—*I've ordered my dinner.*

—*You get to order dinner?*

—*Mom spoils me rotten. I was going to ask for a violinist to come in and play "Bella Notte," but that might be pushing it.*

—*What did you order?*

—*Eggplant parmigiana, with spaghetti.*

—With *spaghetti?*

—*And Italian bread and chocolate pudding for dessert. Mom makes a mean one.*

—*I wish I could join you. I'd bring the Chianti.*

—*I wish you could too, Alex. That'd be so . . .*

—*Maybe someday.*

—(*Singing*) "Someday we'll find it, the rainbow connection, the lovers, the dreamers, and us."

—*I'd give anything for that, all I possess.*

—*Every time I try to tell you exactly what's in my heart, I get tongue-tied. Why is it always so difficult to express*

joy and wonder and emotions. God, Prufrock [A pet
name for A.K.], I'm so lame with emotions!

—*You're a lot better than I am. It's been a curse in my life.*
All my emotions go into my work.

—*That's not true. I know you have emotions, deep ones; I*
feel them. God, that's what keeps me going most of the
time, knowing how much you love me.

—*We all love you, Danny, very much.*

—*It's hard for me to believe, because of all the bad things*
I've done.

—*You haven't done anything wrong, Danny. Bad things*
were done to you, by bad people, but you're a good boy.

—*I need to hear that, I guess. I was so frightened by the*
prospect of making a movie out of my book.

—*Nobody likes to see himself portrayed on screen.*

—*There are other feelings, though, like not wanting to share*
that dark part of myself. And I'm afraid a movie would
tamper with my good memories, the ones that give me
good dreams instead of nightmares. To have someone else
re-create my life would mean that in a way it wasn't mine
anymore.

—*You don't really feel that way, though, do you? Not now.*

—*No, because of you, I don't, not really. I trust you. I have*
confidence in you. Prufrock, you represent some of what
will be left of me after I'm gone.

—*Please, Danny . . .*

—*I only mean you'll be a big part of my life till the end. And*
I'm going to be a big part of yours . . .

—*You already are.*

—*. . . for as long as you remember me. Us finding each*
other was no accident.

—*I believe that.*

—*Over the past few days we've talked a lot about some pretty rotten stuff.*

—*Is that bothering you?*

—*I have mixed feelings about you hearing all those things about me, because you're not mean or heartless so you're going to be sickened by it. I mean, c'mon, I've had sex with grown men.*

—*That was forced on you. Don't dwell on it. It's over, there is nothing you can do about that now.*

—*Knowing you care helps to undo so much of all that. Looking back, I'm thankful that it was never anything that I ever got used to.*

—*You rose above it. You knew you were better and smarter than them. You held on to that. That's what saved you.*

—*My dad said that circumstances can't dictate quality. Good stuff can be found in the worst of conditions, if you know how to look for it.*

—*Bob sounds like a great guy. Do you get to talk to him much?*

—*Not much. I get a few e-mails from him, when he can get to a computer, and once in a while he gets to call. I've talked to him about you.*

—*Oh?*

—*I said you were getting to be, like, another father to me. You know what he said?*

—*What?*

—*He said, A boy can't have too many fathers.*

—*You are like a son to me. Except for the good lines of communication.*

(*Laughter*)

—*I find it so easy to talk to you. Do you mind if . . . if I . . .*

—*What, Danny?*

—Well, I have a dad, but could I call you Poppa? It's okay with Dad. I asked him.

—Danny, I would be proud to be your poppa.

—I have a middle name, but it's one they gave me and I hate it. I'd like to change it to Alex.

—Really? You want to do that?

—If you'll let me.

—Then do it. It's yours.

—Thanks, Poppa. I'm trying real hard to be with you, to stay with you. No matter how bad things get, I promise that I won't give up.

—I won't let you.

—We have a very special relationship, don't we?

—We sure do.

—One that belongs only to us.

—We should enjoy it as much as we can.

—You and I need to do so much together. Neither one of us is ready to call this a wrap.

—Never will be.

—I'll hang on, Poppa, I promise.

15

FedEx told me that deliveries to that address would be sometime between ten and noon. I parked across the street and down from the mail drop, facing Beacon Way and keeping the place in my side-view mirror.

Stakeouts like this, day or night, are always a little harder for a woman, apart from finding a place to pee. Somehow people expect to see a dude sitting alone in his car, but a woman sitting alone in a vehicle is suspect. I lowered the seat back a bit and made myself comfortable. The weather was hovering around freezing but I was bundled up pretty good and had a hot latte grande on the console.

I expected to be there for a couple of hours with nothing to do but wait, so I finally called Walla Walla and got through to the warden. It was a call I'd been putting off since lunch yesterday, and with any effort I could have put it off indefinitely.

Randy Merck was someone I would have just as soon put behind me. Far behind me. He was a rapist, a psycho, a sociopath, a thief, and he had bad breath. Spend any time in a room with him, you want to get hosed down after, and it wouldn't hurt to hose down the room as well. He was now where he belonged and he didn't much mind being there, my opinion. But from the moment I heard Danny's story I was struck by how close it was to Randy's: both rented out to pedophile friends of the family; both tortured, and in the same way; both sexually abused by fathers who wound up in prison for it; both with mothers who disappeared. They could have been brothers. I mean, they could really have been brothers, except for the timing. Randy's father was already long in prison before Danny busted out of his nightmare.

"Hiya, Warden. It's Quinn. Remember me?"

"I won't soon forget you, Quinn. How're you doing?"

Last time I saw him, we watched a fat man hang. My first, but he was a seasoned witness. We didn't spend a minute reminiscing about that.

"You got a package there named Randolph Merck."

He was aware of Mr. Merck.

"I wonder if I could talk to him. I'm working on a case and he might be some help."

"You want to get on his visitors list?"

"No, I sure don't. Who's on his visitors list?"

"You'd be the first."

"I'll settle for a phone conversation with him."

"No problem. Give me your number and I'll set it up and have him call you back."

"When would that be?"

"I'll just have a guard go down and pull him out, take him to a phone."

"Great." I gave him my number. "How's he doing, by the way?" Not that I cared.

"He's a model prisoner. Another year, he's out of here."

I had an involuntary shudder. Next year the country becomes an even more dangerous place. Suffer.

I waited for fifteen minutes, maybe twenty, sipping the hot latte and half-hoping Randy wouldn't call back.

I put my drink back into the cup holder and then raised my eyes. Through the windshield I saw that a man was standing on the corner, my side of the street, and he appeared to be looking at me. Maybe he wasn't. But a man doesn't stand on a corner without looking at something. I hadn't noticed him before. I couldn't say how long he'd been standing there. The wrong kind of tingle danced up the back of my neck.

The man spent a little time searching his pockets and came up with a pack of cigarettes. One of them went into his mouth. The search went on for a light.

I reached for my mini-binoculars and trained them on the tarrying man. I had no problem letting him know I was doing it. He studiously avoided looking my way.

Have you ever seen a person smoke a cigarette and you could just tell he was a nonsmoker? Like in the movies? A smoker inhales with ease, smokes like it's natural to him. Not this yonko. He was using props.

I kept the binocs on him. His hair was black, stringy, and shoulder-length, uncovered in the freezing weather. I wondered if he could be tribal. His body looked stringy, too, his long legs in stovepipe black jeans. He wore athletic shoes. He looked like he had some hard mileage on him, but he couldn't have been more than thirty-something.

He blew on his ungloved hands, looked both ways, and crossed the street, out of my sight.

My phone rang. An operator told me I had a collect call from an inmate at the state pen in Walla Walla.

Randy sounded happy to hear from me. I'm sure he was pleased to hear from anybody. He wasn't all that keen on me last time we spoke.

I kept my eye on the side-view mirror as we talked, checking who was coming in and out of the mail drop.

"Randy, your mother and father were Satanists, ain't?"

"Whoa. What's this about?"

"Not about you, don't worry. I'm just generally interested."

"In Satan?"

"Yeah?"

"Whoa."

"Yeah, you said that."

"So you want to accept the devil into your heart?"

"I'm working on something."

"Glad to hear that, Quinn. Because that's some shit you should stay out of."

"I just want to know a little about how it works."

"Like everything else. The strong have power over the weak. It works the way things are supposed to work."

"Who told you that?"

"My own two eyes."

"It's all about sex?"

"What isn't?"

"Having sex with children?"

"Right. And everyone else. Anything that breathes. Force it and make it hurt."

"Are you still into it?"

"Satanism? I never was into it. I went along with it because it made my life a little easier."

I shuddered again. It was becoming a tic. In the side-view mirror I saw the FedEx truck pull up to the mail drop.

"Who all is involved in it?"

"Like they say . . . legions. In other words, boo-coo peeps, some of 'em in high fuckin' places. You never know when you're talking to anybody if he's one."

"So how do they link up?"

"Oh, there's little things you drop, stuff you can say, after you read some of the signs."

"What signs?"

"Look for a small scar, close to the eye, or on the lip. And then walk away, Quinn. These are fuckin' evil people."

"I don't want to dreg up old shit, Randy, but remember when we X-rayed you, and they found those pins and needles?"

"Hell, Quinn, relax about it. I don't hardly ever think about it anymore. I live for the day."

"Considering where you spend your days, that's a pretty good trick."

"Nothin' I can't handle."

"Tell me you were the only little boy who ever had to go through all that stuff."

He laughed. A laugh like that comes from, where?

"What are you, a missionary? That's a land you don't want to bring your Bible to. Bring a .357 Magnum. Better yet, a fuckin' stake; hammer it through their fuckin' hearts."

"Right. And the thing about renting out little boys . . . ?"

"And girls. Fuck one, fuck the other, it's all young meat."

It was freezing outside and I'd lost the heat that was in the car, but that's not why I shivered.

"So it happens. Often. Not just to you."

"Messin' up kids, it's what they do best. Not that they don't get off on it, but there's good money in it, too."

"In the name of Satan?"

"Oh, fuck, Quinn, Satan just gives it a hook and a history."

Over the top of the side-view mirror I saw a woman turn the corner and walk toward me, on the other side of the street. A knitted cap covered her head, and a quilted coat her bulky body. Her walk was that slow rolling waddle common to the morbidly obese. Between the cap and the scarf, a round face with plump red cheeks was visible but hard to make out. She walked with her face turned to the storefronts, either window-shopping or catching her own reflection.

"How do you beat them? Randy?"

"Ain't it clear? You don't. You stay clear of them."

"Listen, Randy, sorry, but I have to go. I might call you back."

"Why don't you just come visit me, Quinn? We can sit down and chew the fat. Bring me some smokes, okay? I can tell you all kinds of good shit."

"Yeah, I'll get back to you."

I picked her up again in the mirror as she passed me. Even under the coat her huge rolling buttocks were visibly keeping up a rhythm. I had the sense, for no particular reason, that she didn't get out much. She seemed a little lost. She turned into the mail drop.

The phone was still in my hands. I had Alex Krapp's numbers on my speed dial now. I gave him a call.

"Give me Danny's number, Alex, okay?"

"I'm fine, how are you?"

"I'm busy here, I don't have time for the niceties. Forgive me. The number, please?"

"Sorry, Quinn, I can't do that."

"Come on. I'm working for you."

"I promised his mother. Nobody gets his number except through her."

"I'm looking at his mother, or at least I was until a minute ago."

"Really? Where are you? Why do you need the number?"

"I can't run every little thing by you. You have to give me a free rein or I'm boxed in."

"I'm sorry, but I have parameters. I have to respect them."

The woman, who I was sure was Celeste, came out of the mail drop carrying a FedEx envelope.

"Look, I don't have time to argue with you. If you won't give me his number, call him yourself. But it's got to be now."

"And say what?"

"Anything. Has he called you today?"

"Not yet."

"So call him."

I tossed the phone into my purse and got out of the car. I tailed her from the other side of the street until she turned the corner, when I made a diagonal to her side. I stood at the corner and watched her waddle to the bus stop in front of the Mexican hair salon. She stopped and waited with a few other people, one of whom was the tall, stringy dude I'd just had the binocs on. Okay, so where's it say I can't be a little paranoid?

Now I stood on the same corner, blowing on my own hands, pretending not to be watching anything.

I could go back and get the car, but following a bus in a car starts to look like a parade after the second stop. I put my purse over my shoulder, my hands into my pockets, and went to wait for the bus, wherever it was going.

Krapp's Cassette #DT-9 (partial)

—*Hello?*

—*Hey, Prufrock.*

—*Danny, my boy, how're you doing?*

—*Vic says that if we're careful we might have an easy day.*

—*I'll keep my fingers crossed.*

—*Toes too. (Laughter) Mom's gonna make a great pasta dinner, and I plan to be a real slob with it.*

—*Good, put some pounds on you.*

—*I try. Thanks for yesterday . . . and last night . . . and all of this other time that we've spent together.*

—*It's my pleasure, don't you know that?*

—*Somehow I've always known that this is the way things were meant to be in the world. This is the way people were meant to be with each other. Loving, not . . . you know. It's not about material things or possessions or anything like that. It's about coming away with a very full heart because someone loves you a lot.*

—*I'm beginning to find that out, too.*

—Maybe things in the past have been crummy and things in the present are inconvenient, but I'm still very, very aware, and grateful, that there are those in my life who have not been in the lives of other people who are two or three times my age.

—What do you mean?

—That some people don't get to know the love I have, no matter how long they live. They never get to know. When I'm down, I think about all those people. Can I have a hug?

—Sure, kid, hold on. Are you holding me?

—I'm holding on. When I'm feeling down or cynical I remember that a hug is a circle of open arms to hold in love and keep out harm.

—I'll remember that.

—Mom always says that when all is said and done, all that matters is love. I want you to know you're loved, Prufrock.

16

CELESTE SAT ON ONE OF THE FORWARD SIDE SEATS DESIG-nated for the old and the handicapped. I took a seat midway back. The tall, stringy man sat in the rear of the bus. I decided to give him a name. Stretch.

I kept Celeste in my line of sight. The FedEx envelope sat on her lap. She looked at it from all sides but did not open it. Since it was addressed to Danny, she probably wanted him to open it. The bus rolled along Beacon Way.

My phone rang. Her head turned to the sound, along with a few others, the way everybody does now when a phone rings in places one never used to. I bent forward, got the phone out of my bag, and answered. It was Alex calling me back.

"Okay, I called but I got the answering machine," he said.

"And what does that usually mean?" I said, as low as I could.

"Unfortunately, that he probably had to go to the emer-gency room. It happens frequently."

"Okay."

"That's it?"

"Right."

"Will you call me as soon as you find something out?"

"Sure."

I shut and stowed the phone. Did I lock the car? I couldn't remember. All I would need is to go back and find my ride stolen.

Celeste got off the bus at the fourth stop. So did I. So did Stretch, which I was wishing he wouldn't.

I followed her farther on down Beacon Way, inventing reasons for slowing my pace. Her gait was so slow I could have kept up with her on my knees. Stretch, though walking none too fast either, passed me and then her.

On Hind Street she turned right. I stopped at the corner and watched her walk up the slight incline. It was a quiet residential street with very little car traffic and no foot traffic, except for Celeste. I crossed the street and paused on the other side to check her progress. Well, this was awkward.

I hung on the corner like one of the professional panhandlers that abound in Seattle. A step this way, a step that way, marking my turf. A block away, Stretch stopped. He was lighting up another cigarette and looking my way. I stared right back at him. You looking at me? He turned his head and continued walking.

Mentally, I pushed Celeste up the hill. She made the first intersection at last and I was able to walk up the other side of the street with space to spare by the time she crossed. Once again I had to hang back. I waited until she was mid-block before I crossed. I was greatly relieved to see her turn toward a house, open the gate, go up to the front door, unlock it, and step inside.

I walked on past her house, a small, white, clapboard place surrounded by a four-foot chain-link fence with a gate, the kind of fence you'd expect a pit bull to be kept behind.

There was no porch, just a concrete stoop of three steps and a vinyl canopy well past its warranty. The windows were small and covered with closed venetian blinds. On the roof I noticed a chimney and a satellite dish. No garage, no driveway.

I kept walking to the end of the block, with a much-quickened pace, circled around, and went back to the bus stop, this time going in the other direction. I checked the schedule posted on the pole. I had maybe ten minutes to stand in the cold. I was going to call Alex back but decided against it.

A Quiznos was half a block away, so I went and grabbed a classic Italian sub and a Diet Coke to go and used the bathroom while the kid built the sandwich.

For the past couple of years public restrooms have been for me decompression chambers, withdrawal centers, cooling stations used to mop the sweat and keep my head from exploding, but there I was, doing what comes naturally, freaking out neither myself nor others. I hadn't had a hot flash or a message of mortality for . . . how long? Since last night on the plane. It seemed longer. Maybe I was coming out of that particular passage of life. I had, after all, felt that little twinge where a twinge ought to be felt.

I grabbed my sandwich and ran for the bus, catching it just before the door hissed shut.

As the bus pulled into traffic, I glanced out the window. Stretch was standing inside a video shop, watching me.

"Stop the bus!" I yelled.

"Sit down, lady," the bus driver barked at me. "I can't stop in the middle of the road."

"Pull to the curb!"

"Not till the next stop. Sorry."

I was being tailed.

17

MY CAR WAS WHERE I'D LEFT IT, SAFELY LOCKED. I DROVE back to Celeste's house and made a pass along the nine-square-block area surrounding the house, chasing my tail. No Stretch.

Danny had told Alex that Vic got all the ice to battle his fevers from the gas station on the corner. I noticed, though, that there wasn't any gas station on the corner, nor on any corner in the area. I parked across the street from the house, at the end of the block, where I had my sandwich and listened to *Fresh Air* on NPR.

I had no doubt I was being tailed, and it felt creepy. Suffer myself. Poetic justice. Live by the sword, die by the sword. Physician, heal thyself. Like that.

Assuaging any moral qualms, I reminded myself that the people I tailed, at least, never knew I was following them.

After the creepiness came anger, frustration, and, okay, a smidgen of fear. I was left with the question: who the hell would want to follow me?

As I ate my lunch, neither tasting nor much enjoying it, I rifled mentally through my past cases. This was only my second year as a PI, but I'd already worn out several pairs of Rockports, metaphorically speaking. Really, the damn things never wear out.

In brief, I've offended some people: husbands and exes; boyfriends, girlfriends, and thwarted suitors; embezzlers and their brothers-in-law; distant fathers and wayward daughters; distrustful Manny, vindictive Moe, and conniving Jack.

The thing is, I have faces for all of those people, and Stretch didn't match any of them. I went back to my original question. Why would a stranger be following me?

If Satanists are as organized and as vicious as Randy seemed to believe, and I figured he ought to know, then there was an outside chance that Stretch was the devil's emissary. He looked the part.

But how could they even know about me? I was spanking new to the case and the only one who had any knowledge of me was the man who had hired me, Alex Krapp. And possibly his secretary, Gwendolyn. And, of course, anyone with the smarts to tap into his telephone. If Satanists have infiltrated all walks of life, it's a certainty that some of them work for Verizon.

Okay. New deal. Start seriously looking over your shoulder.

I bagged up what was left of my sandwich and tossed it behind me, onto what was becoming a rather unkempt backseat.

I always carry a set of phone books back there, both white and yellow pages. Stacked, they provide just the extra inches I might need to get my eyes to window level. They're also ready kindling should I suddenly need a fire. Swung well, the white one makes a dandy blunt instrument. Held over the heart, with all the luck in the world, the yellow one could stop a bullet. And of course there is the original and intended purpose: finding phone numbers.

If I lived in this house, I thought, and had a sick kid with an emergency, where would I go? Swedish or Harborview. I called Swedish first. I sounded worried but still back from hysterical.

"I just got a message that my nephew was taken to an emergency room, but my sister didn't say which one. His name is Danny Timpkins . . . or Daniel Timpkins. Is he there in your hospital? He's fifteen; he's got AIDS and respiratory problems and high fevers. Has anyone matching that been admitted this morning?"

Well, of course, she wasn't going to tell me. I would have to appear in person. Would she tell me then? No, but I could wait in the waiting room. For what? She had no idea.

I called Harborview. This time I was hysterical, and this time it was my son. He was taken while I was at work. I wept, I screamed, I threatened lawsuits. I gave them enough information to overcome any confidentiality qualms. No dice.

There were a few other hospitals I could have called but I was sure I would get the same response.

I gave Alex Krapp a call. It went right to message. He was probably sitting on his dock watching the tide roll in. If so, he was freezing his ass, as I was.

I had to restart the car and let it idle just to get warm again. I must have nodded off, not a smart thing to do in a running car. The ringing of my cell phone woke me up. It was the screenwriter returning my call. I looked at my watch. Three o'clock. It was starting to get dark.

"Danny called me back," he said.

"When?"

"Just ten minutes ago."

"I left a message a couple hours ago."

"Yeah, I was at lunch with Joanna Cassidy."

"Who's she?"

"An actress I know. She's got a job in Vancouver, so she stopped to see me."

"I never heard of her."

"That is not my fault, Quinn."

Da frick.

"What was she in?" I asked.

"*Blade Runner.* She was the sexy dancer in the clear plastic raincoat running away from Harrison Ford until he blew her away."

Woi Yesus. I did remember her. She was beautiful. And age-appropriate.

"So how was your lunch?"

"My lunch? Fine."

"Long lunch, huh?"

"I usually take a long lunch, if I'm with somebody."

"I had mine in the car. I wasn't with anybody. Sandwich from Quiznos."

"You eat fast food?"

"You got a problem with that?"

"Why would I have a problem with what you had for lunch?"

"It sounded like something."

"Quinn? It was like asking you if you smoke. Like, why? What's going on with you, anyway?"

The hormonal war being waged inside of me inflicts collateral damage. Wild ricochets. After some skirmishes, entire squads of reason go missing in action.

"Excuse me," I said, "I'm sorry. I have a condition that aggravates itself. It makes me a tad cranky."

"I understand."

You'd almost think that he did. Just his saying it soothed me. I got back on track.

"So you talked to Danny?"

"Yes, they took him to the emergency room middle of the night. His lungs were filling up and Vic couldn't do anything about it at home."

"What hospital?"

"Saint something or other. He goes to several different hospitals. I just call them, collectively, The Big House. He gets a kick out of that. He hates having to go to the Big House. In fact, we've been talking about his next book, which I suggested he call *Stories of the Saints,* about his experiences in the hospitals he goes to. They steal from him, they say horrible things, as though he weren't there, like he has no right to go on living. And the crowd that passes through the ER in the middle of the night is pretty colorful. Drag queens, addicts, Goths, a wide range of characters. I urge him to keep writing. I think it's what's keeping him alive."

"Saint something?"

Seattle is a secular city. It tolerates God, but it doesn't hang a lantern on Him. I never heard of a Saint something hospital.

"Can you find out the hospital?"

"Yes. I can ask about that."

"Do that. Did he say anything else?"

"About what?"

"About the hospital. What did they do to him there? Who was with him? Did he go by ambulance or—?

"He never goes by ambulance. They take him—either Celeste or Vic, usually both. They have a big Chevy Suburban."

I scanned their side of the street. A dirty gray Suburban was parked two doors away. It looked about ten years old and was showing some wear.

"You'll be talking to him again today, ain't?"

"I'm sure I will."

"Ask him if it was Celeste who took him to the ER today. If she was along, or was it just the doctor took him."

"All right. What are you after?"

"Did he tell you anything else, about his day?"

"He said they stopped and got a pizza to take home. That's usual, too. They stop and get him a treat of some sort. He loves Italian food, including the desserts. Or some candy. He loves See's and chocolate of all descriptions."

"Isn't all that a risk? I mean, if no one can get in to see him, how do they take him outside?"

"Very carefully, apparently. There's a whole prophylactic protocol they have to go through. It's quite involved but they have it down. They have to. Except for the roll-in into the hospital, they keep him in the car."

"Did he say where they stop? What pizzeria or restaurant? Any landmarks?"

"I never asked. It never seemed that important. Is it?"

"Not by itself."

"What do you mean?"

"This counseling center Celeste runs? You said it was a storefront. Did she ever say what neighborhood or where it was, any landmarks there?"

"No, only that she's turned it over to volunteers since Danny came into her life. She just uses it as a mailing address.

As I told you, they're very secretive. They can't let those people find Danny."

"It's not that hard. I found him in half a day."

"You did! That's fantastic!"

He was excited, as much as I'd ever heard him. I was sorry I'd pumped him up.

"Not him, but where he lives. Same difference, ain't, if I'm a bad guy? I'm parked outside his house right now."

"Really? What are you doing?"

"Not torching it—which I could if I was one of Satan's little helpers, is my point. Listen, Alex, does anyone else know you've hired me?"

"God, no. Why?"

"What about Gwendolyn?"

"I never told her. What did you tell her?"

"That I was a consultant on marine law."

"Marine law?"

"She asked and I came up with something."

"Well, I never told her anything about you."

"Then there's no way she would know?"

"I don't think so. Why do you ask?"

Then I remembered. When Gwendolyn took off her glasses, I noticed a small scar next to her right eye.

"Woi Yesus," I said aloud.

"What?"

"I'll get back to you, okay?"

"Quinn, what's going on?"

"Not just yet, okay? Gotta go."

"Okay. But please, don't let Danny find out you're working for me."

"Don't worry."

"Or anyone else for that matter."

"That's what I'm talking about."

And then I did it again. I swear, sometimes I'm a stranger to myself, maybe even a danger to myself. "Alex, it's none of my business who you have lunch with."

"It never occurred to me that it might be."

"I needed to find you, and I got impatient. I apologize."

"Forget about it."

—*Never go to the ER on a Saturday night.*

—*I'll do my best.*

—*Every loose nut in the Northwest rolls in there on a Saturday night.*

—*How'd it go? Apart from the nuts.*

—*I had an allergic reaction.*

—*To what?*

—*God knows. They pump me so full of different crap, and everything runs the risk of an allergic reaction or an infection. And they talk about me like I'm not even there. I guess they think I'm so out of it I can't hear them.*

—*Who?*

—*The orderlies are the worst. One of them said I was a "waste of resources." He thought I was taking up too much air and food and water.*

—*Jesus, Danny. The guy's an asshole.*

—*Yeah, I know, but it gets me to wondering.*

—*Stop it, Danny. You have a life to live, just like anyone* else. Who's to say you won't live longer than that stupid orderly?

—Thanks, Poppa. Sometimes I get so confused. I'm glad I have you to straighten me out.

—Tell me what you're going to get for dinner.

—Ah. Fried mozzarella and zuc for the main course. Baked lasagna, stuffed shells, and baked manicotti. Dessert: chocolate fudge layer cake, chocolate pudding with whipped cream.

—What, no wine?

—(Giggles) Vic keeps promising me, one of these days, but he never delivers.

18

NIGHT FALLS SO EARLY IN JANUARY, YOU MIGHT AS WELL SKIP lunch.

By the time I finished talking to my client I was sitting in darkness. A light came on in Celeste's house. I hadn't seen any of the neighbors outside of their houses where I could talk to them like a lost visitor looking for a particular family: a "heavyset" woman, a husband named Bob who is serving in Iraq, an MD boarder, and a teenage boy who is very sick. The kind of family you might notice.

Outside, it was getting even colder. I was about to call it a day and go home, but before I could start the car, Celeste's front door opened. A man stepped outside and buttoned up his wool coat. From my vantage point I couldn't make out all the features, but I'd put him at about six feet, two hundred pounds. He wore a Navy watch cap. I couldn't tell how old he might be, but he had a bit of difficulty coming down from the stoop.

I watched him open the gate and make his way to the

Suburban. He lifted himself inside. His slowness did not come from age. The man had a prosthetic leg, the left one. From the way he moved, it seemed he was still getting used to it.

I dropped to the seat so that I wouldn't get caught in his headlights. Then I made a U-turn and followed him.

Even a klutz can tail a big lumbering Suburban, especially when the mark has no reason to suspect he's being followed. Unless, of course, he *did* have a reason to suspect someone might be following him. I'd soon know.

He led me back down the hill and hung a left on Fourth Avenue. Somewhere past the Pink Elephant Car Wash, he turned off and I followed him to the TS Tavern, tucked away among the aging warehouses of the area. When he pulled in to the tiny parking lot, I went on and parked farther down. The whole area was deserted.

I have this flashlight, about the size of your middle finger, that can light up a Beach Boys concert in the park. I flashed it into the Suburban. A sleeping bag was laid out on the backseat, with a pillow at one end. Nothing else told me that anyone was living in the vehicle, so it looked like it could be doubling for an ambulance.

The TS Tavern was warm, at least, and although like at any other bar there were regulars, strangers drew scant attention. It was a workingman's bar, as familiar to me as the post office, the kind of place my old man used to take me to, to watch the fights on TV, me and Toby, the rat terrier. In those days, in that place, dogs were welcome pretzel catchers in any bar in town, and there were a hundred and sixteen licensed bars in Shenandoah, in an area one mile square. You could say I grew up in a culture of alcohol. Sounds worse than it was. In fact, it was pretty good.

Though not a sports bar by design, the joint boasted two

HDTV sets hanging from opposite ends of the ceiling, one showing college basketball and the other showing golf from California, without irony. In the new century, the working-man has come to embrace golf. This should not confuse me as much as it does: I have a vivid and unsettling memory of a high-stakes croquet match one Sunday afternoon among miners and truck farmers and volunteer firemen that fell into dispute, transforming the mallets, the wooden balls, and even the stakes into lethal weapons. Drink played a part.

My person of interest had to be Doctor Vic. He sat alone at the bar, apart from a cluster of regulars that included a couple of boozy broads past their prime. The regulars were all of that age when discussions inevitably turn to who is about to die next, from what not entirely unexpected disease or injury, and who among them were likely candidates, given the assorted and untreatable chronic pains they all suffered.

A medical authority sitting just feet away would not have been excluded had he been known to them. For his part, Doctor Vic showed no interest and volunteered no recommendations for their relief. Truth be told, he didn't look like a doctor. He lacked a certain professionalism. I should talk.

I took a seat three stools down from him, even farther away from the doomfest. I don't know what a doctor is supposed to look like. If there is a mold, Vic, according to Danny's story, broke it anyway. Harley rider. AIDS victim. Street-easy. But I didn't see much of that, either, in this yonko. I was close enough now to see that he might still be in his thirties. He looked that young, but I figured if he had been Celeste's classmate he must be older.

He sat with both arms on the bar, taking in no more than his pint of Miller Lite and Jager shot. He looked troubled, but not sick. I always assumed that you lost weight behind AIDS, but Vic was twenty pounds over. I wondered, can you ride a Harley with a replacement leg, the shifting leg? I'd have to ask someone. Could be that's how he lost the leg in the first place, but you'd think that would be part of the story. I grew up with the legless, the armless, the fingerless, and those guys all loved to tell the story, which often involved total ignorance of, or a momentary lack of respect for, the physics behind operating a Harley.

I ordered a Ballard Bitter and pretended to check messages. I turned the phone toward Vic, without turning myself, and took his picture.

Then the damn thing rang.

Vic looked toward me. I put the phone to my ear and turned away.

"Yeah?"

"It's Alex."

"Wuz up?"

"I talked to Danny again. He said it was Vic took him to the ER. Celeste didn't come along."

"Why not?"

"She had errands to run, and Vic assured her it wasn't life-threatening."

"Okay."

"I also asked him the name of the hospital, but he said Vic never tells him the name. He makes one up, as a gag. St. Elmo's, St. Otto's, St. Vinnie's, like that."

I was trying to imagine what my end of the conversation might sound like to a stranger. So far, it sounded like an undercover cop, so a little embellishment was in order.

"Just set the oven for three-fifty," I said, putting an edge to my voice, "and slide it in, uncovered. Is that so hard? I'll be home before it's done."

"What?" Poor Alex. I had already laid the groundwork for my instability, now I was sealing the deal. But I'd forgotten he was a screenwriter. "Oh, you can't talk, right?"

"Yes, like that."

"Okay, I'll talk to you later."

"You got it."

I gave a glance to my side. Shit. He was still looking at me. And not in a nice way.

"Sorry," I said. "I hate it when people use phones at bars."

He shrugged and turned back to his beer.

"Used to be you could get away for half an hour, have a quiet drink on your ownie. Those days are gone," I said, pressing for a little conversation.

"You could always turn it off," he said.

His voice was a whiskey bass. Reminded me of home.

"I would, but I've got a sick child," I said.

"Then what are you doing here?"

"Hey, don't make me feel any worse than I already feel."

"A sick boy needs his mother."

"I didn't say it was a boy."

"Hmm. No, you didn't."

"It is, though. My son. My adopted son." How far could I go with this, I wondered, without sending up a red flag? "Actually, it's my husband's kid from his last marriage. Sometimes it's more than I can handle."

"A kid is a great responsibility, a full-time job. Especially when he's sick."

I leaned toward him and extended my hand. "My name's

Irene Fetterman." I appropriated the name from an old classmate, the one who made the cheerleading squad.

He looked at my hand for a moment before shaking it. His grip felt substantial.

"Yeah, pleased to meet you," he said, then turned back to his beer and waved for another Jager. End of conversation.

All I had in mind at that point was waiting him out, see how long he stayed, see if he got drunk on those Jager shots. After the third pint I was getting a little buzzed myself. I was going to have to go sit in the car again and pick him up when he left the joint. I would have, too, except for the blonde who came in and stood just inside the door for a moment, acclimating herself. Unlike me, she was not at home in places like this.

She wore a faux fur hat, which she took off to give her short-styled hair a shake. Most men would find her easy to look at. For a moment I thought she recognized me and was going to say hello. She walked straight toward me, taking off her coat, showing off a pretty good figure. Who am I kidding, I'd kill for it. She sat on the stool next to my mark. He turned and said, "How did you know I was here?"

His voice had changed. Now it had a strange, almost imperceptible lift to it, like a man very pleased to see a woman he shouldn't be seeing at all. I looked for a ring on her finger. There wasn't any, though, let's face it, the things aren't glued on.

"Danny told me you were here," she said. The feeling in her voice almost matched his. A little waver, a touch of excitement. She was glad she had found him but knew she shouldn't have been looking.

"Yeah, well, he shouldn't have."

"Don't blame him. He wouldn't have told me if he didn't want you to see me."

"You want something to drink?"

"Thank you. I'll have a cosmopolitan."

"Hey. Look around you. This guy knows how to mix whiskey and soda."

She laughed a little, leaned toward him to bump shoulders, and said, "Then I'll have a glass of white wine. Is that doable?"

"That's doable," he said, and I could catch his smile. It put her face in a glow.

He took their drinks and moved to a booth eight feet behind me. I could catch their reflection in the mirror, but I couldn't hear their conversation. At one point he put his hand over hers, but after just a few seconds withdrew it again.

I sorted out what I knew, or at least what I'd heard from Alex Krapp. Vic was a Harley-Davidson doctor, an old friend and classmate of Celeste, a tough guy with a soft interior, a bisexual who, by the way, had AIDS. He'd given up his practice to tend full-time to Danny. I guess I had assumed that was his whole life now, but obviously he had a little something going on the side.

I ordered another beer, which would render me somewhat less than a hundred percent. Less than 75 percent.

Vic got up and out of the booth, which was a bit of a struggle for him, and walked down the dim hallway to the toilet.

I moved fast. I put in my earpiece and flipped open my phone.

The only two booths in the tavern were separated by a raised tabletop, probably for the free Monday night buffet of buffalo wings. The *Times* and the *Post-Intelligencer* and *USA*

Today were spread across the surface. I started talking a line of nonsense and slid into the booth opposite the woman, on my knees and riffling through the papers.

"Just hold on a minute," I said. "There's a paper right here. Okay, we can catch *Notes on a Scandal* at the Egyptian. Well, what do you want to see? No way am I watching guys getting shot in the head again. I'm sick of that Scorsese shit."

I aimed the phone at blondie and took a picture.

"Okay, so it's the Egyptian. Cool."

I pulled the earpiece out and shut the phone. I left a tip on the bar and beat it out of there before Vic could get back.

At my car, I realized I shouldn't get behind the wheel. A DUI could wreck my career. Not to mention maybe my car, some innocent bystanders, and my own self. I called a cab and waited. I wasn't thrilled about leaving my pretty PT all night in this neighborhood, but some things can't be helped. I leaned against the car and chilled, literally, like some shunned hooker.

A black Ford Explorer using only the parking lights slowly rolled toward me. I could hear the deep bass beats of some hip-hop. The volume went down as the car pulled closer to me. My hand went into my purse.

The car inched past me and then stopped. Close enough to put me in the red glow of the brake lights, far enough away so that I could not see into the car. My hand was firmly on the LadySmith. I backed away, went around my car, and put it between me and the Ford. I tried to memorize the license plate number, but the beer had fogged that particular talent. I was sure it had diminished my shooting talent as well, which was never better than C-plus in the best of circumstances.

The hip-hop volume went up again. The headlights turned on, and the Ford pulled away.

Krapp's Cassette #DR-4 (partial)

—*I got a blow job once watching one of your movies.*

—*(Krapp's laughter) Was he that bored with the movie?*

—*It was a chick. I think your movie inspired her.*

—*I hope this was on DVD and not in a theater.*

—*Was that wrong?*

—*(Krapp's laughter) Well, I'm glad I could help. Is it true a bisexual can always get a date on a Saturday night?*

—*(Vic's laughter) Only dweebs go out on Saturday night.*

—*What I don't understand is lesbians.*

—*What's to understand?*

—*How do they know when they're done?*

—*(Both laugh) That's an interesting question.*

—*So how do you decide who to, you know, go out with.*

—*Me, it's just a preference, at the time. What I like in a woman, I like in a man, and the other way around.*

—*But physically . . .*

—*Just a preference. Like black or white or yellow or brown.*

*You can love 'em all but kind of wind up preferring one
over the other. Me, I prefer men. You ever do it with a
man?*

—No. I'm a hopeless heterosexual.

—I knew that. Since Bob's over in Iraq, you're the only real
male model Danny has.

—I don't know, you're a pretty good model.

—You know what I mean. [A well-known psychologist]
thinks Danny is gay.

—No way. He really likes girls. The little guy's never going
to have one, but I know he likes them.

—It breaks my heart.

—Yeah. Mine too.

—It's hard to believe that there's a God who would let a
little boy endure what Danny's had to.

—I wonder about that, too. Sometimes it keeps me awake at
night.

—When they busted his father and searched the place they
found all this kiddie porn. After we took him home, and I
came to live with them, this cop I knew gave me a DVD.
He said Danny was on it.

—Oh, Jesus . . .

—I didn't play it. I kept it hidden high on a shelf, behind
some old books. I never even told Celeste. Then one night
Bob and I were sitting around here, talking about all
kinds of stuff, and we decided to play it.

—Don't tell me, please.

—Don't worry, I won't. Bob and I went nuts. Neither one of
us owned a gun, thank God, because we wanted to go out
and kill someone. But who? The father was already in
jail. He'll never see the light of day. The others? Who

knows where they are. We were up all night. Too much in
a rage to sleep. And then we hear the whimper of this
sweet little boy, Danny, having a nightmare.

—How does he do it?

—I wish I knew. He's one in a million.

19

In the morning it was cold but dry. The forecast was for rain, but weather forecasting in the Pacific Northwest is an inexact science. I warmed my hands on my latte as the old elevator slowly took me up to my office.

That blonde in the bar last night looked like a girlfriend. Maybe a little uncertain, still, maybe less than licit, but some kind of romance was in the air.

(Mom, Dad, I've met a man. A doctor! He has only one leg and AIDS and he prefers men, and, oh, he lives with a quarantined patient, so we won't be able to live together, but I know he's the one.)

Danny had told the blonde that Vic was at the bar, which meant she was in communication with the kid, as were enough others, apparently, to keep the boy's call-waiting clicking continuously. The backseat of the Suburban looked rigged for carrying a sick child, but even the child didn't know to which hospital, sainted or otherwise. An adoptive father in Iraq, on a secret mission. An adoptive mother who runs a counseling center through a mail drop and struggles to get through a doorway. And all of them in the sights of vicious and vengeful Satanists. The only thing I could disprove was that the counseling center was in a storefront. I couldn't prove anything.

Ninety-seven middle schools in Seattle take on the task of molding the minds of the presumably malleable. I eliminated the alternative schools, the private schools, and the Catholic schools; it would be too difficult for Danny to go unnoticed in one of those. He could have gone to one of the schools in the boondocks, but I gathered from his story that he was at home on the city streets. I was guessing he was from close to the downtown core.

I took a calculated guess on the neighborhood he might have grown up in. I drove out to Mercer Middle School on South Columbian Way.

They linked me up with a vice principal, a nice enough lady but forged with the hard edge her position demanded. I put her at ease by telling her that I, too, once attended a middle school, though in those days it was known as junior high. I was sure the nomenclature had been changed to protect some sensitive souls from feeling subordinate to anything. Back then, we didn't have graduations from kindergarten, elementary school, or middle school, thereby making the graduation from high school something solemn and special. Hell, we didn't even have a vice principal. Our town figured principaling was a one-man job.

She wasn't terribly amused by my reminiscing.

Before I ever stepped into the school I tried to come up with who would be doing this. Social services? Graduate student doing a thesis? Long-lost relative? Novelist? In the end I settled on what comes easiest: the truth. I flashed her my creds and told her I was a detective on a case. Nobody's fool, she actually read them. There is far too much radar today to hope to fly under all of it.

"Private detective?"

"Yes, ma'am."

"All right. How can I help you?"

"Within the last three years, there might have been in your school a boy, an excellent student, but badly abused by his parents. He would have disappeared abruptly, and—"

"You're talking about that boy who wrote the book?"

She stopped me cold. "So you know about him?"

"I've read the book. It's a wonderful, life-affirming story. I even thought about suggesting it as supplemental reading for our eighth-grade English classes, but I'm afraid it would be too controversial."

"The sexual abuse?"

"Yes."

"Was he a student here?"

"No. A reporter came here a month ago . . . no, just before the Christmas break, asking the same question."

"A woman?"

"Yes, she said she was from *Vanity Fair* magazine."

I thanked the lady for her time and motored.

I could check all the other schools and the hospitals as well and find I was weeks behind Eve Gosler. To get to the bottom of this, I was going to have to do what she couldn't. Of course, it would have helped to know what she had already done.

After a hot link at Pecos Pete's, I went back to the office and used my cold line to call *Vanity Fair* in New York. I got

an intern—you can hear it in their voices—who told me that
Eve Gosler was out of town. He couldn't tell me where she
was.

"Yeah, I know where she is," I said, "but I don't have her
number. She's supposed to interview me, but I don't know
when or where. On that story about the kid."

"If you give me your name and number, I'll have her call
you."

"Terrific. My name is Grace Johannson."

I gave him the cold line number and hung up.

If the story was true—and I had scant reason to believe it
wasn't, even though all the details weren't hanging together
very well—and if the names were changed and the records
sealed, the only way to finger the kid would be through an
eyewitness, someone who actually knew him.

Seattle isn't that big but it's still big enough for a kid to
disappear in, which I guess could be said for any city in the
country, given as a people our general character of transience.
People come and go. Yes, but someone always remembers.
The book was a minor best seller in the Northwest, reviewed
well, with a couple sidebar stories. Celeste, after all, was a
local and known, even if keeping a low profile. She gave a
couple interviews, in print only, requesting a respect for her
son's privacy, and the story just sort of drifted away. But
someone always remembers. "There was a kid like that in my
class. . . . I remember him from GameWorks. . . . He used to
hang around the Public Market, listening to the buskers. . . .
My son played with a kid like that who one day just disappeared."

Until I could find someone who remembered Danny in his
earlier life, the best way to approach him, I thought, was
through his adoptive mother, Celeste.

I spent the rest of the afternoon working a title search on Celeste's address. Sergeant Beckman had already traced the plate on the Suburban for me. It was hers.

The house had been owned free and clear by John Volinsky, a Bremerton shipyard worker. Celeste's father. She inherited the house, along with a settlement, when he died in a shipyard accident in 1988, but I discovered that she didn't inherit it outright. Two brothers, Eugene and Timothy, signed quitclaims giving her the house. She has lived in it ever since.

I did a search on her two brothers. Nothing came up for Eugene, but Timothy turned out to be the owner of a high-end men's clothing store named, what else, Timothy's. I knew the place. It was a Seattle fixture. It was the kind of store where during their big January sale you could find a shirt reduced from three hundred dollars to two-twenty. I used to buy my ex's clothes and I don't think I ever paid fifty bucks for a shirt. I kind of miss buying clothes for a man, but you're always going to be missing something, ain't?

—*How's your day been going?*

—*I was on the computer all morning.*

—*Doing what?*

—*Well, first I played some chess with a guy in Minnesota.*

—*How'd you do?*

—*I beat him.*

—*You play poker?*

—*Sometimes, but not for money.*

—*How do you do at poker?*

—*Pretty good. I can remember all the cards.*

—*Let's go to Vegas?*

—*(Giggles) I'd love to go.*

—*We could break the bank at the Mandalay.*

—*Then I got all involved in something else.*

—*Oh?*

—*Poppa, you gotta help me with this.*

—*What's the problem, son?*

—*After I played chess, I had a long chat with Ginny, online.*

—*How is she?*

—*She's back at school now. We chatted for a long time.*

—*Yeah?*

—*Real personal stuff.*

—*Yeah?*

—*Then she said, Let's get on the phone, so I called her and we talked on the phone. A long time. About everything.*

—*Yeah?*

—*Poppa. (Long pause) She said to me, she said, "I love you, Danny."*

—*Wow.*

—*I know. I didn't know what to say. It wasn't like when you and I say it, or when I say it to my mom. This was serious. No girl has ever said that to me.*

—*She beat you to the punch, kid. I know you love her, too.*

—*I do, even though she's in college and everything.*

—*Well, she's only a freshman, and you're as smart as she is. Smarter. What did you say?*

—*Oh, God. I'm such a dork.*

—*C'mon.*

—*I said Thank you.*

—*Yep, you dorked out.*

—*Poppa. Give me a break.*

—*Call her right back, admit you were scared, and tell the girl you love her.*

—*But I have no right to do that.*

—*Says who?*

—*I'll never be able to take her anywhere.*

—*Again, says who?*

—*C'mon, Poppa, I'll fight till the end, but we both know I'm gonna lose.*

—We all lose in the end, Danny. What counts is what we do in the meantime.

—But what can we do? I mean, Ginny and me.

—Look, whatever you've been doing, it's made her fall in love with you, and you with her. So keep on doing that.

(Danny crying)

—Is this a good cry?

—Yeah, Poppa.

20

SUKI STARTED BUILDING ME A SAPPHIRE BLUE MARTINI AS soon as she saw me come through the door. You've got to get to Brasa early on a Friday night. Come at six-fifteen and there's no more room at the bar for a girl to sit alone and enjoy some of the best food in Seattle, at happy hour half-price.

I hung my coat over the back of the bar stool and settled in. The ice-cold gin hit my lips, pleasantly numbing them.

"Got anything interesting going?" Suki asked me.

She is an Asian girl, in black and white, always, with severely short hair, really just a suggestion of hair. Men like to look at her. Women too. Me, I enjoyed watching her work. She owns whatever space she's in, a professional.

I showed her the photo I had of Danny Timpkins.

"Cute kid," she said. "Is he missing?"

"Not really. Just very hard to see."

"You're not going to see him in here."

"No, but a girl's got to eat."

"What can I get you?"

"The paella, but let me spend some quality time first with your handiwork here."

She smiled and went off to juggle several drink orders at once.

The cranky old lady from the Y came in and ordered her usual bourbon, water back, putting her pack of Winstons on the bar. In two sips, she was stepping outside for a smoke. She would do that two or three times before she finished her drink. She wouldn't leave a tip, she'd complain about the price, and then she'd go, back to her room, and I'd wonder if I might ever turn out to be her.

Twelve people, men and women, coworkers probably, sat at one of the long tables, laughing, enjoying their after-work drinks.

I went down into myself a little. Down there, I said, I don't want it, I don't need it. Honestly, though, I missed the human touch. I could have used a hug once in a while, a little kiss, a tender hand on my breast. Suffer.

I took out my phone and put in a call to the screenwriter.

"Good evening, Quinn, I was hoping you'd call me."

"Thought I'd check in."

"Glad you did. What have you got?"

"You home alone?"

"Yeah, why?"

"It's Friday night, I thought you'd have a date for dinner."

"Quinn, it's five-thirty. Later, I'll put together something. I don't want to leave the house."

"Yeah, I'm gonna have a drink and a bite and wrap it up myself."

"So where are we?"

"Where are we? Well, there's no storefront service center, just a mailbox. And I don't know if it means anything, but Vic has only one leg and a girlfriend—"

"Get out."

"I'll send you her picture. His too."

"I've seen pictures of Vic, but I can't believe he has a girlfriend."

"It looks pretty new."

"It's possible, I guess, but . . . he hardly ever leaves the house, except for an occasional bike ride or a trip to the hospital."

"She talks to Danny."

"Who?"

"Vic's girlfriend. She talks to him."

"Really? Danny never mentioned her."

"I also learned that Celeste inherited her house from her father. She has two brothers."

"I knew about the brothers; she talks about them. Didn't know about the house, though."

"She didn't say one of the brothers lives with her, did she?"

"No. One owns a clothing store. That's Timothy. The other, Eugene, is in the Army, in Iraq or Afghanistan."

"What about Danny? Did he have any biological siblings?"

"He's mentioned a brother, and a sister, though the sister is a little murky. One day this little girl showed up at the house and he was told she was his sister. They doted on her for a few months and then she disappeared. You can only imagine what Danny thinks happened."

"What happened to the brother?"

"I don't know—he was already out of the house by the time Danny made his escape."

"Major creepiness, Alex."

"Yeah, I know that. It's a miracle Danny survived, let alone turn out to be the kind of boy he is."

"I ran Victor D'Amato's name through the AMA rolls. Not there, buddy."

"No, he wouldn't be. He's using a different name."

"Why?"

"I told you."

"The avenging Satanists? But Celeste is pretty visible, and there she is on the dotted line, Celeste Volinsky Manfred Timpkins."

"But I don't think those are her legal names."

"Some of them are. Volinsky is. Celeste is. I have a contact at the local Army Reserve unit. I asked him to expedite a records search on Vic, along with Bob Timpkins, through the Department of Defense. I'm waiting to hear back from him, but I'm betting we don't get a hit."

"Probably not. Bob changed his last name, too, for the sake of Danny's story. I don't know his real name."

"Called back into the service? Secret mission? Can't come home till it's over over there?"

"That's the way I hear it. Between you and me, Danny tells me it's putting a strain on the marriage. She can only do so much."

"She's got Vic."

"It's not the same."

"All right. Hang up, I'm going to send you the pictures. Call me back on my cell phone."

My man at the Army Reserves is a tightly wound captain

who hired me once to tail his wife, which I did with some mis-giving because I was worried that if she was fooling around the captain would empty a clip in her. Turned out she wasn't having an affair but was going to weekly Al-Anon meetings. I sat him down and had a motherly with him, told him the truth: he had a good woman, but he was going to wreck everything if he didn't square up. He must have taken the ad-vice to heart. They're still together, and he thinks he owes me. I don't take advantage of it.

Sergeant Beckman is another matter. He damn near got me killed through his own stupidity. It was an isolated inci-dent. He's a pretty smart guy for a cop, but the call was as close as you can get, so he does owe me big-time and we both know it. Him, I take advantage of.

He took the stool next to me.

"Good evening, Sergeant, let me buy you a drink."

"I'm still on duty. Maybe a Jack and soda."

Which for him was like, what? Iced tea?

I gave Suki a wave and watched the sergeant scope her out as she mixed his drink.

"Pull your tongue back in," I told him.

"I can look."

"You can look but you can't drool."

He got his drink and we clinked glasses, mine nearly empty now. We drank to truth and justice.

"I went back three years," he said, "and I couldn't find any matching case, nothing near what you laid out. There are some guys in the joint for similar raps: incest, sexual abuse, ritual sexual abuse. Murder, even, but the timing is all wrong for you. These cowboys have been on the shelf for a long time."

"Thanks anyway."

My paella arrived and I ordered a glass of Spanish white wine.

"That looks good," said the sergeant, his nose hanging uncomfortably near my plate.

"You want to order something? I'm buying."

"No, I'm on overtime, gotta go to the Sonics game."

"On overtime?"

"The governor's going to the game. I'm adding some security for her."

He finished his drink.

"Enjoy the game," I said, "and thanks for nothing."

"Anytime."

I smiled. It's good to have a friend on the SPD.

I waited for him to leave the bar before putting in a quick call to Bernard's cell.

"Bernard, where are you?"

"Key Arena. Where you at?"

"Still have that ticket?"

"No, sold that one. Now I'm buying."

"What have you got?"

"Two close to the floor. Not as close as the one I tried to sell you. Why, you suddenly want to go?"

"I do."

"Fuck me."

"What? I can't change my mind? Hold one of those tickets for me."

"Yeah, and what should I do with the other one, eat it?"

"Go ahead and sell it. You got plenty of time."

"No way, man, if I can unload 'em both to a couple, they're gone."

"You're a real friend, asshole."

"I'm in business, Quinn."

"All right, I'll take them both."

"First you don't want any ducats, ever, then you want two a time. My curiosity is aroused."

"Just hang there until I show up."

I folded my phone and got back to folding my paella inside of me.

So where's Alex? I wondered—he was supposed to call me back. I saved the hunk of chicken for last. I sliced it fine and forked it up with the last of the spicy rice, washing it down with the wonderful chilled wine. When I finished I ordered an espresso, since it appeared my day was not over yet.

I called Alex Krapp back.

"Hello, Quinn."

He sounded different, a little down.

"The picture came through okay?"

"Yeah, it came through fine."

"So our gay doctor's turned queer and hooked up with a girl, huh?"

"Quinn . . ."

"What?"

"It's Eve Gosler. The woman is Eve Gosler, the reporter."

"Well, that's different. I suppose the reporter could meet the doctor for a drink, but this wasn't an interview, trust me."

"Yeah, well, that wasn't Vic with her."

"What?"

"The picture you sent me. It wasn't Vic. The picture Danny sent me of him is a different man."

Krapp's Cassette #DT/CT/DR-247 (partial)

(Wheezing sounds, gasping)

—Danny, listen to me. Make some noise.

(More wheezing, gasping)

—Knock something off your end table! Do it!

(Crashing sound, glass breaking, wheezing)

—(Celeste's voice in b.g.) Vic! Vic, hurry! (Picks up phone)
Alex, is that you?

—Yes, Celeste, thank God you heard him. He can't
breathe.

—Vic, it's Alex, he said Danny stopped breathing.

—(Vic's voice in b.g.) Ask him how long.

—Maybe a minute.

—(Celeste) A minute, he says. Vic, you're hurting him!

(Crying)

—Stay with me here, Celeste. Vic knows what he's doing.

—He's pounding his chest! Vic, you're going to break
him!

—*Stay with me, Celeste. Don't worry, Vic's on it.*

—*Oh, God, we're going to lose him. Oh, no . . . (Wheezing sounds in b.g.) He's digging into his throat!*

(Unidentifiable sounds in b.g.)

—*(Vic in b.g.) Danny, you don't have to do this, buddy. You want to go, it's all right. If it's too much, you don't have to do it anymore, buddy. You've done more than anyone. Just let it go, buddy. It's all right.*

—*God, Celeste, don't let him . . . (More wheezing in b.g.) Celeste? Celeste, talk to me!*

(Long pause)

—*Celeste?*

—*He's breathing, Alex. Some color is coming back.*

—*God!*

—*(Vic in b.g.) C'mere, Celeste. Hold his hand. Talk to him. (Vic on phone) Alex?*

—*Yeah, hi, Vic.*

—*Hi, buddy. Am I good or what?*

—*Is he all right?*

—*He's alive.*

—*God!*

—*You okay?*

—*Me? What happened?*

—*He shut down. Breathing stopped. Went into a panic. Heart flatlined. I'm treating him for shock; I'll ease him back to sleep in a little while. (Sounds of Celeste cooing, Danny breathing, coughing) I've got him in the oxygen tent. Don't worry, I'll keep an eye on him. Let me put the phone to his ear, you can say good night. (Pause) Danny, I'm gonna put your poppa on . Don't try to talk.*

—*Danny . . . Danny, it's your poppa. You're a good boy,*

and I love you. You're going to be all right. Everything's fine. We've got to cast for your movie, you know, so get some rest and then back to work tomorrow, okay?

—(Vic on phone) He smiled. Can you believe this kid? I'm glad you were here with him, buddy.

21

I LEFT BRASA AND SAW A FAMILIAR BLACK FORD EXPLORER parked across the street, the same vehicle that had spooked me outside the TS Tavern. Being tailed was beginning to piss me off. I tried to dash across the street, but there was too much traffic. I hurried to the corner and had to wait for the light. By the time I was able to cross, the Ford was pulling out and moving down Third Avenue. There was no way I was going to catch it, but I was close enough to read the license number. I wrote it down on my palm.

I took a cab back down to Pioneer Square. Since all the traffic was going in the other direction, on First and Third, toward the Sonics game, traffic was light on Second Avenue.

Neither Alex nor I had an explanation for why the investigative reporter would be having drinks in a blue-collar bar with a man I tailed from Celeste's house, a man who could have been Vic. Or someone else. But strangers were not allowed in that house. No one was allowed in that house. Let's say it was Vic, and the picture Alex possessed was of some unknown person. That Vic and Eve might talk was not so surprising—she was doing a story and he was a principal. But what I saw was not an interview. It was a rendezvous. Even though Vic was blindsided by it, he didn't seem to mind too much. If they weren't lovers, they were on the cusp, and this is an area with which I have a little experience, and the intuition of my gender. We know when a line is about to be crossed. We've seen it happen with men who were supposed to be bound to us. We've seen it happen to ourselves, and wished we could back up. Once the line is crossed, though, there is no way back. Only forward, if you're lucky, and now lugging a weight you never wanted to carry.

But let's say the man in the bar wasn't Vic? Who was he and why was he leaving Celeste's house and driving her car? And worried about seeing that woman.

I went up to my office and checked my cold line. Eve Gosler had left her cell number. I called.

"Hello?"

"Hi, this is Grace Johannson."

"Oh, hi, I got your message. Was I supposed to interview you? Because I have no record of that in my notes?"

"That was a ruse. I'm sorry. I'm a private detective, covering much of the ground you already have. You're looking to prove the kid doesn't exist, I'm looking to prove he does. So why don't we help each other."

"And who are you working for?"

"Nobody you know."

For a moment I wasn't sure we were still connected. Then: "Well, it looks like your job is done. My story's been spiked."

"And by 'spiked' you mean . . . ?"

"Killed."

"Oh? Why is that?"

"I've seen the boy. He's for real. So I've got no story."

"Then all that the family has claimed is pretty much true?"

"Pretty much. Most of the finer details don't pan out, but much of that is deliberate red herring."

"To throw off the Satanists?"

"The who?"

"The Satanists out to get Danny and anyone around him."

"Satanists are out to get them?"

"I don't know. I don't know what Satanists do."

"You brought it up."

"Just passing it on."

"It would explain a lot."

"What do you know about the biological father in prison, and the adoptive father overseas?"

"I haven't seen or talked to the biological father, but I did talk to Bob, briefly. He called me from somewhere in Iraq. He's a guy under a lot of stress."

"And the surrogate father, Alex Krapp? The one Danny calls Poppa?"

"He's a well-known screenwriter. I've met with him."

"What about that live-in doctor? Victor D'Amato?"

"He's for real. He's what's keeping Danny alive. And the mother is a saint. I've never met anyone quite like her. It all smelled bad to me in the beginning, and so I pursued it as an exposé, but sometimes even I'm wrong."

"I was told nobody could see the boy, too risky all the way around. The boy in the bubble. So how did you manage to see him?"

"In the bubble. I saw him in the hospital, in the ER."

"What hospital?"

"Harbor General. Though Vic and Danny call it Saint Ce-cilia, I don't know why."

"How did that happen? You in the hospital."

"The family was frustrated and annoyed with me, so they called and told me to come to the hospital. I stood several feet away, masked and gowned."

"You talk to him?"

"Briefly, just to make sure it was the same voice I'd heard on the phone."

"And it was?"

"It was the same voice. Even the speech patterns. It was Danny, and he is quite a kid. A prodigy, really. I was im-pressed."

"Yeah, he seems to have that effect on people."

"You've talked to him, then."

"Kind of. When did you see him at the hospital?"

"Yesterday."

It sounded right to me. While I was tailing Celeste, Vic was with Danny at the hospital. It sounded right, but my gut told me something was way hinky.

"So, Eve, who was at the hospital with him?"

"Miss Johannson . . ."

"Grace, please."

"Grace, as I said, I'm satisfied. The story is dead. Danny is alive and real. So it would seem that your job is done, too."

"It would seem."

"Let's leave these people alone."

"Gladly. I just like to have all my details pass muster. Like in a court of law."

"None of this is ever going to be in a court of law."

"Fine by me, but you're a reporter. All your details have to line up, or why would they bother paying some newly minted liberal arts grad peon wages to be a fact finder?"

She gave me a little laugh.

"What details are you interested in?" she asked.

"Like, who was at the hospital with the kid?"

There was a pause. It made me uneasy. If it made her uneasy, I couldn't sense it in her voice when she finally said, "The doctor was with him."

"You mean Vic?"

"Yes, and there was another doctor, a pulmonary specialist, and a nurse."

"Celeste, the mom, wasn't there."

"I didn't see her. She might have been somewhere else in the hospital, the cafeteria maybe. I didn't ask. I was there for just a minute or two."

"Okay. So I guess we're both on to the next thing, ain't?"

"The next thing?"

"The next story, the next case. This one's done."

"Yes. Yes, it is."

"So why are you still in Seattle?"

Again, that pause.

"I wanted to see the new sculpture park before I went back to New York."

"Yeah, that's a big hit. Everybody wants to see the new sculpture park. I've got a free day tomorrow, I can show you around."

"You've seen it?"

"Hey, just because I go snooping in the night doesn't mean I can't appreciate a nice hunk of granite sitting on its bad side."

"I'd take you up on the invitation, but a friend has already volunteered."

I was dying to spring it on her that I'd seen her sipping white wine with Vic D'Amato at the TS Tavern, but I didn't want to blow my cover and it wasn't going to get me anywhere anyway. She'd claim it was a professional meeting and I'd have to argue with her about what professionalism looks like. After I argued the point with myself.

I couldn't find a hole in her story. On the other hand, it might have been all hole and no story.

The avenues were jammed so it made no sense to take a bus or a cab to Key Arena. I walked back downtown and stood in line for the Monorail. Once I was on board, that beauty had me in the Center in less than two minutes. The ride took long enough for me to call Alex and give him the good news, if I felt like it, but I could do that anytime. Like after I talked to the governor.

I hurried to the front entrance of the Key Arena, burning off some of the paella . . . and the martini . . . and the wine.

Bernard was in motion, in a thinning crowd, hawking the two tickets he was supposed to be saving for me.

"For you, forty bucks," he said.

"Have a heart, Bernard, the game's already started."

"That's why I'm reducing the price. First five minutes don't mean shit anyway."

I gave him two twenties and snatched the tickets out of his hand. A black kid around twelve was hanging by the doors, hoping someone would drop an extra ticket on him. I did him the favor.

"Hey, thanks, lady."

"Sure, enjoy the game."

I wasn't waiting for him. I dashed into the arena. The tickets didn't live up to Bernard's promise. They were closer to the ceiling than the floor. I wormed my way down. I spotted Sergeant Beckman in one of the entryways. I scanned the crowd several rows down and saw the governor and her party, three rows up from the court. I headed in that direction. None of the ushers gave me any grief.

One of the things I've always liked about the Northwest is the accessibility of its movers and shakers. I wasn't in town for a week before I was introduced to the mayor and chatted with him about how the salmon were running. In Spokane I once had pancakes a table away from Governor Lowry, asked him to pass me the boysenberry syrup. One morning, I let Bill Gates have the last old-fashioned donut at Starbucks.

I knew I could park myself in the aisle and eventually fall upon the gov, but why waste time when I had the sergeant?

"What the hell, Quinn, are you tailing me?"

"I got no interest in you, Studly, but I need to pose a brief question to Her Honor."

"What kind of question?"

"Don't worry, it's professional."

"Forget about it."

"One minute. Next time-out."

"No."

"Okay, end of the quarter."

"You're skating on thin ice, Quinn."

"C'mon, don't make me get tough with you."

"Ha!"

"I can smell the Jack Daniel's on your breath, officer."

"Fuck you, Quinn."

"You wish."

We rolled the log another minute or two, until he caved, as we both knew he would. I waited with him for the first quarter to end.

I showed him my palm and had him copy down the license number of the black Ford Explorer.

"In your spare time," I said.

"Who's this?"

"I'm hoping you can tell me. He may mean me harm."

"Oh, we couldn't have that."

"My feeling exactly."

"So you don't understand sarcasm, do you?"

"I do, but sometimes I ignore it."

We watched the game. One white guy was on the court. He looked eager to please.

"So how's the wife?"

"Dunno. I hardly see her. I should have you tail *her*."

"You worried?"

"Who's she gonna get better 'n me?"

"Dunno. Never saw the lady."

"She's a babe."

"There you go."

"She's carrying about twenty extra pounds, after the kids."

"Some dudes like that."

"I don't mind it much myself."

"Since you're carrying thirty."

"Fuck you."

"You want me to check her out? I'll give you the secret admirer discount."

"Admire? I don't even like you."

"Full price, then."

When the teams converged on their benches for the first-quarter break, Beckman led me down the stairs to the governor's row. He leaned in and whispered something. She in turn whispered to the aide next to her, and he vacated his seat for me.

I sat down and said, "Thanks, Your Honor, I'll be out of here in a minute. Celeste Timpkins, who worked on a project with you when you were lieutenant governor, a project involving abused children, has asked you to vouch for her adopted son, Danny, who's become kind of controversial. Her name at that time was Volinsky or Manfred. What I want to know is—"

She stopped me. She had no idea what I was talking about. She didn't know Celeste or Danny, nor could she remember the project for abused children. I thanked her, apologized for the interruption, and beat it out of the Key Arena.

Outside, the kid I'd given the free ticket to was loudly trying to hawk it.

—*Believe me, Alex, if anyone could see Danny, if we were
willing to take the risk for anyone, it would be you.
You're all he talks about. I don't know if you realize it,
but you're keeping him alive, as much as Vic or I.*

—*No, it's Danny, his sheer force of will.*

—*Don't underestimate the power of love.*

—*I know the money doesn't mean anything to you, but . . .*

—*It doesn't. I'm not going to put my son at risk for a
hundred thousand dollars.*

—*It doesn't mean anything to me, either. I mean, I get paid
whether they make the movie or not, but it is such a good
story, such an incredible story of redemption and love. I
know Danny is uncomfortable being an inspiration, but
imagine the good his story could do, for all those other
children out there, to raise the consciousness of a people
that tend to forget the helpless. All it would take is my
coming face-to-face with Danny. For a minute. Thirty*

seconds. HBO says that's all they need to green-light this
movie.

—Oh, God, Alex, sometimes I . . . I would never ask you to
say something that wasn't true, but it would be so easy to
just—

—I can't do that, Celeste.

—I know you can't. You're a good man. I wouldn't ask
you to.

—So what are we going to do?

—Obviously, they're not going to take Vic's word, or
anybody in my family's. Would they take the word of
someone well-known, someone highly placed who stands
to gain nothing from it?

—Who do you have in mind?

—Well, several years ago I did some work for the lieutenant
governor of Washington. I helped her on a special project
involving abused children. We've stayed in touch since
then, and when all this happened with Danny, when he
first came into my life, with all that happened afterward, I
called her. By that time she had been elected governor.
Anyhow, I asked her for some pretty big favors and she
was just wonderful with helping to speed everything
along. She had them make a deal with the father so that
there wouldn't be a trial, and then she was able to seal all
the records and arrange for a change of names. I haven't
been in touch since then, but I feel sure she would help. I
could call her and ask her for one last favor. She could
vouch for Danny and his story. Would that satisfy HBO?

—I don't see why not. It's an excellent idea. I'll run it by
them.

22

I TOOK THE MONORAIL BACK DOWNTOWN, AND WALKED AS fast as my Rockports would move me to Timothy's on Seventh Avenue. A clotheshorse was just locking the door as I got there.

"Sorry, we're closing."

He was good-looking, well-groomed, and blatantly gay. Even with the employee discount, he had about three grand on his back.

"Sorry, I'm not shopping. I need to talk to Timothy himself."

He spoke into a mini-walkie-talkie he wore on his belt. "Timothy, there is a woman here to see you."

I heard the man's voice crack on the walkie-talkie. "What's her name?"

"Eve Gosler," I said, "from *Vanity Fair.*"

The clotheshorse tried not to be impressed. He relayed the information and Timothy told him to bring me up.

I followed him to a back room and was led into Timothy's

office. I shut the door behind me as Timothy rose from his desk.

"You're not Eve Gosler."

What the clerk wore? Double it for Timothy. Six grand, easy, from shoes to cravat.

"Eve is off the story. I'm Grace Johannson. I'm her replacement."

"Not a problem, I hope."

"No, happens all the time."

"When will the story run?"

"Out of my hands."

"But you'll give some good mention to the store?"

"Prominently, of course."

"Please, sit down."

Buying and selling. Sometimes I have to think that's all there is. I took out a notebook and sat down.

"You and your brother quitclaimed the house your father left you all to your sister, ain't?"

He looked at me a little funny, like maybe I wasn't a reporter.

"Yes, that's true."

"How come?"

"I didn't need it or want it. Eugene was making the military his career so he didn't need it, either. We knew that Celeste did. She'd never lived anywhere else. We didn't take any of the settlement, either. We hoped that with the house and the settlement Celeste could—"

"Could what?"

"Have a life of sorts."

"Well, wasn't she married then? With two girls?"

"You're a little confused. Didn't Miss Gosler tell you? The girls are mine."

"Jenny and Leslie?"

"Yes, they're my daughters. I know she loves them, but I don't know why she claims they are hers."

"Have you asked her?"

"As I told Miss Gosler, we don't talk."

"And what about Celeste's husband, Mr. Manfred?"

"Who?"

"Manfred."

"My sister was never married. She was always very shy and withdrawn. And there was the weight thing."

Timothy himself was thin. He looked good in clothes.

"No men in her life?"

"None that I knew of. I'm a little uncomfortable talking about Celeste, frankly. We have a . . ."—he looked for the right word—". . . strained relationship."

"I understand." Which wasn't going to keep me from asking the questions. "I'm sure high school was no picnic for Celeste."

"She had a terrible time in high school. I loved it—played sports, was on the student council. Anyway, it didn't go much better for her in college."

"She went to college?"

"Junior college. Seattle Community. I pretty much fell out of touch at that point. I send her some money on her birthday and holidays."

"So you never met her husband. I mean, the current one who's off in Iraq? Bob Timpkins?"

"No." He was uncomfortable. A little squirmy.

"You know how they met, though?"

"I heard."

"You sound like you have some doubts."

"Let's just say I've never met the man."

"And little Danny, her adopted son? Have you met him?"

"I've heard about him."

"But never saw him?"

"No."

"You haven't read the book?"

"No."

"No interest?"

"Not really. As I said, we're not a close family. Look, most of this I already told the other reporter."

"Indulge me. You mind? So your brother, Eugene, is, what? In the Army, Navy . . . ?"

"Was. He was in the Army. He intended to make it a career, which I think would have been perfect for him."

"Why's that?"

"He's a good guy—smart, patriotic, loyal. But he needs a structure. He thrives in a disciplined structure."

"So why did he get out?"

"Courtesy of an Iraqi bomber. He lost a leg."

"What did he do in the Army?"

"He was a medic. Truth is, he could have been a doctor or a nurse. He still could be. He has the intelligence, but something else is missing."

"What?"

"I don't know. But I'm sure it was left in Iraq."

At the very least, I now knew Vic D'Amato's true name, and his true relationship to Celeste and Danny.

"Would you say your relationship with him is strained?" I asked.

"Do we talk? No. But he's my brother and I love him. And I love Celeste. I find I just can't be around them, separately or together. I'm embarrassed to say it, but there it is."

"Families," I said, as though that said it all.

"Yes," said he, knowing what I meant.

"Did you tell all this to Eve Gosler?"

"More or less."

"You've been very cooperative, then."

"I have nothing to hide."

"Unlike your sister and brother, ain't?"

"As I said, I don't see them anymore."

"Thanks, Timothy, if I may."

"You're welcome. Let me know when it's published."

"Will do. One more thing. Is your brother gay or bisexual?"

"No, he's always liked women, and they've always liked him."

"Does he have AIDS?"

"What? AIDS? No, of course not. At least I've never been told. God, I hope not."

"I wouldn't worry about it."

It was bitterly cold by now, but I decided to walk the ten minutes to my office.

Since Celeste was lying about *every*thing, what were the odds, I wondered, that she was telling the truth about *any*thing? And if she was telling the truth about the one thing—Danny—why would she have to lie about everything else?

On weekends, Pioneer Square is a lot like Bourbon Street, except for the girls flipping up their halters and flashing their boobs. Simply not the climate for that sort of thing. You could hear the cacophony before you arrived at it: the yeow boys and the trilling girls, throwing caution to the pigeons, the music pumping out of the bars, the buskers pounding the street. My office was smack at the gateway to the show.

I saw that my three Indians were happy with the attentions of four or five American studies majors, who were giving them a small honorarium for their lore. I waited a minute in the cold for the kids to move on before I made a slight detour to their bench and said, "What would it take to get you three into a cheap hotel tonight?"

They looked at each other with glazed eyes, then back at me. David said, "We like you, Quinn, but not that way."

Clifford said, "I could like her that way."

I gave him a slap upside the head with no real force.

"Woi Yesus, don't make me puke, okay? All I'm saying is I'll give you the money to get you out of the cold tonight. I don't want you freezing to death."

"You could just give us the money," David said.

"No cash, just the room."

They conferred for a minute and told me they preferred the pergola. It wasn't all that cold, they thought.

You can't make street people do what they don't feel like doing. It's pretty much the only thing they can call their own.

I unlocked the side entrance to the Pioneer Building and went up to my office.

The clamor of the street still reached me there. The light was blinking on my answering machine. It was my captain from the Army Reserve unit.

"Hey, Quinn, I ran that name, Robert Timpkins. Yeah, he saw combat duty, but it was in Normandy, World War Two. Nobody by that name in Iraq. Hope it helps."

Sleep would be a bitch until the bars closed. Besides, I was still processing the espresso I'd had at Brasa. I thought about calling Alex, but why wreck his night's sleep, so I stayed awhile in my office and played some of his cassettes.

Krapp's Cassette #CT/DT-127 (partial)

—Hello?

—Hi, Celeste, it's Alex.

—Well, hello. I haven't talked to you for a long time. Danny hogs the phone whenever you call.

—You could get a second line.

—What good would it do, you'd still spend all your time talking to him.

—You could get on the extension.

—Oh, no. We don't do that around here.

—Do you want to let him have his own phone? I'll pay for it.

—Thanks, but no, I couldn't.

—Why not?

—We're okay.

—You sure?

—Moneywise, we're doing fine. We keep our expenses real low.

—Except for medical expenses.

—*It's all covered. We don't have to pay a cent for Danny's
care.*

—*Anyway, I'm happy to help.*

—*You've done so much already. By the way, thanks for
giving Danny that iPod. That was so sweet.*

—*It's nothing.*

—*He opened the box, and I wish you could have seen his
face. His eyes went wide, and he said, "Mom, can I keep
it?"*

—*Well? Can he?*

—*We had a little discussion about it. I said, "Well, he is
your poppa now. I guess you can accept a gift from your
poppa."*

—*I was so bummed when he told me someone at the
hospital ripped off his.*

—*They tell you not to bring anything valuable, but . . .*

—*I just had to replace it. He has to know there are more
good people in the world than bad people.*

—*That's a lesson that's hard for him to absorb, all he's been
through. Do you want to talk to him?*

—*Sure. But it's been nice talking to you, too.*

—*Yes, we have to do more of that. Danny?*

—*(Danny's voice, distant) Yes, ma'am?*

—*Your poppa is on the phone.*

(*Pause*)

—*Hi, Poppa.*

—*Hey, buddy.*

—*Thanks so much for the iPod.*

—*You're welcome. Did you notice there was a song already
on it?*

—*I almost peed my pants!*

(*Celeste's voice in b.g., laughing*)

—*Sorry, Mom, I didn't know you were still here.*

—*(Celeste in b.g.) I'll go make dinner and let you boys talk.*

—*She called you* boy. *How do you like that?*

—*Even though I'm years older than her.*

—*Not that many years. You look younger.*

—*(Laughter) I sent you an old picture. So how did you like
the song on the iPod?*

—*(Imitating) "Oh, no-o-o-o-o!"—"MacArthur Park." It
cracked me up. I've played it a dozen times.*

—*You're a glutton for punishment.*

23

SOMETIMES I UNPLUG THE PHONE, JUST ON THE OFF CHANCE that I may have to wake up to its ringing after it's taken me half the night to fall asleep. Some people wake up to a gentle touch and a whisper. I'm not one of them. Suffer. That night I'd forgotten to pull the plug.

The phone rang. I squinted at the clock. Nine-thirty. You could say I slept in. I didn't feel like it.

"It's Alex."

Just that much told me his mood was down.

"I was going to call you," I said. "Last night. But the moment passed."

I could hear the compressed sound of traffic in the background.

"Where are you?"

"I'm downstairs. Can I come up?"

I was already bounding out of bed, grabbing a fresh pair of panties.

"Would you mind bringing me a latte? There's a Star-bucks just to your left, on the corner."

"Yeah, I saw it. What would you like?"

"Latte, double-tall nonfat."

"Caramel or something?"

"No, nothing sweet."

"Cinnamon?"

"Just the latte, thanks."

I scurried around my bedroom, hoping there was a long line at Starbucks this morning. I hastily made the bed, gath-ered up teacups and strewn clothing, and quickly had the place looking more than the personal disaster it usually was.

Swirling mouthwash, I gave the bathroom a lick and a promise. I washed my face and laid on a thin coat of pale lip-stick and a tad of blush. My hair was hopeless, so I just slapped on a head wrap. I pulled on a sweater and squeezed into a pair of jeans. I hurried to the living room to check my-self out on the mirrored wall. My feet were bare, but they may be my best feature so I left them that way. I looked like a retro flower child late for the sing-along.

I was wiping down the kitchen when he called back. I buzzed him in.

"Eighth floor, left off the elevator, then a right."

"I remember," he said.

I opened the door and left it ajar while I made a last-minute inspection of where I lived. It would have to do.

He gently tapped on the door frame.

"Hey, c'mon in."

I didn't know whether to give him a handshake, a light hug, or an air kiss, so instead I gave him an ambiguous wave: come in or go away.

He was wearing a flannel-lined fawn suede jacket and

what looked like a hand-knitted scarf tied in the French manner. His hair, like mine, was all over the place, but on him it was sexy, made him look like a windblown poet. He held a cardboard take-out tray on which were two tall lattes and a white paper bag in which I hoped was at least one old-fashioned donut. Proust had his madeleine, the ex-cop has her donut. Under his arm was a folded newspaper.

We sat at my small glass table by the window.

"You have a nice view. I mean, during the day as well."

"If you like brick and cobblestones."

"Who doesn't?"

"Not me."

"You even have a piece of the water."

"The place was advertised as 'water view,' which technically is true. It suits me. I'm here for a while."

"I love your confidence."

"Oh, yeah, I'm a born optimist," I lied.

"Optimism is the madness of wisdom. Cynicism is the wisdom of madness."

"Tops on or tops off?"

"Let's be elegant," he said, and removed the tops from both coffee containers.

I took them to the kitchen and threw them in the trash bag below the sink.

"This is a pleasant surprise," I said, sitting down again. "What's in the bag?"

He split it down the side. An old-fashioned donut. I tore it in half and bit into it.

We spoke at the same time.

Him: "I'm going back to LA Monday."

Me: "What's the word on the governor?"

"The governor? You mean, on vouching for Danny?"

"Yeah."

"She's still mulling it, according to Celeste. Everything is politics, and some stuff sticks to you. Deep down they're all afraid of being human."

"Oh, she's human enough. I talked to her last night."

His head snapped up. "How'd that happen?"

"It's a long story. I bumped into her at a Sonics game. She never heard of Celeste or the kid, nor of the special project, or sealing any records. Nothing."

He took a sip of his coffee and stroked his chin.

"Could be she's playing it very close to the vest."

"This isn't Hollywood. She wasn't playing anything. She just didn't know what the hell I was talking about. Doesn't matter anyhow."

"It doesn't?"

"I've got good news and I've got bad news."

"What's the good news?"

"I talked to Eve Gosler. She's spiked the story. Guess why?"

His eyes showed some glitter. "She saw Danny?"

"At the hospital. Talked to him, too. So she's satisfied there's no story, no hoax."

"Quinn, that's fantastic news."

"Ain't it?"

"I'll get HBO to call *Vanity Fair* to verify and we can get into preproduction. It'll be such a boost for Danny. Fantastic!"

"Don't you want the bad news?"

I could see he didn't but that's the deal with good news/bad news.

"Okay," he said. "What's the bad news?"

"I don't believe it. I don't believe Gosler ever saw the boy. Weird as it sounds, I think she fell for Vic and got co-opted."

"Just because you saw them having a drink together? That's pretty flimsy."

"By the way, Vic doesn't have AIDS and he's not gay and he's not even Vic. His name is Eugene. He isn't a doctor, either, though he is a friend of the family. In fact, he's pretty much what's left of the family. He's Celeste's brother. The other brother has washed his hands of them. Eugene came back from Iraq one leg short, adrift, sad, and looking for a hook to hang his life on. He's probably got some PTS disorder. Celeste created this whole new world for him and he signed on. He had nowhere else to go."

"He has to be a doctor. He's diagnosed me over the phone and my own doctor confirmed."

"He's an ex–Army medic, so he knows his way around some stuff and has nothing but time to study more of it. Nothing checks out with this crowd, Alex. There's no Bob Timpkins in Iraq, there's no father in prison, no mother on the arfy-darfy, no service center, no hospitals, no schools."

"But all of that—"

"Yeah, I know. Names have been changed, records sealed. It's all bullshit. She doesn't have two daughters, she has two nieces. She's never been married. She's hardly been out of the house—I mean, for years and years. Not since junior college, and I'm going to look in on that. Think about it. The boy writes a book, he's in the papers a couple times. Wouldn't somebody come forward and say they knew the kid? Some teacher? A classmate? Anybody? People who hire me, Alex, aren't always happy with what I tell them, and now you're one of them. I'm sorry."

He stood up, looked at himself on my mirrored wall, took a slow turn around the room, and stopped at the window, where he put his hands on his sides, over the kidneys, as though recovering from a double punch to the vitals. He looked down at the street. My Indians had survived the night, still under the pergola, keeping awake by identifying the makes and models of passing cars.

"The love I feel from Danny . . ." he said. "How he's touched me in a place no one ever has. Are you telling me none of that is real?"

"The love may be real, but I'm telling you there is no Danny."

"That just can't be."

I wanted to put my arms around him, and I wouldn't have minded having his around me, but I kept my seat.

"In your scenario . . ."—he was still looking down at the street—"who am I talking to when I'm talking to my son?"

"Celeste. I played the cassettes you gave me, half the night. I've been listening to them off and on, but last night I paid real close attention to Celeste and Danny. Didn't you ever hear the similarity in their voices?"

When he turned from the window, the edges of his mouth went up a bit in an attempt at a smile. He sat down again and sipped his coffee.

"Their voices aren't anything alike," he said. "Not even close."

"We could have them digitally analyzed. It's not cheap, but it would tell you . . . if you really want to know."

"Quinn, there are three people living in that house. I don't have any explanation, any *good* explanation, for all the other things you've discovered, but of one thing I'm sure:

There are two adults and one very sick boy living in that house. And it's a daily struggle to keep that boy alive. I'm positive of that. Hell, I'm part of it."

I didn't say anything. I'd pretty much said all I could.

"Look, Quinn, I've talked to all of them, at the same time."

"On different extensions?"

The screenwriter thought about it for a moment.

"They don't use the extensions, not together. It's all about giving Danny his privacy and as much independence as they can. Celeste explained it to me."

"Okay."

"You don't believe me."

"I don't care."

"One night I was talking to Danny. He was having trouble breathing, and then there was silence. First wheezing, gasping, and then silence. I was in a panic, but I tried to keep calm. I told him to knock the stuff off his end table. Celeste and Vic came running in. I was on the phone while Vic was working on Danny. I was terrified that he was going to die while I was on the phone, that we were all seeing him through his last moments on Earth, but I did my best to calm Celeste and then I was on the phone with Vic while Celeste was talking to Danny. I was talking to all three of them, in a moment of great crisis. It wasn't a charade. It couldn't have been."

"Yeah, I heard that cassette."

"So you know what I mean."

"Listen to it again, closely. You never hear Celeste and Danny talking at the same time."

He stroked his chin again. He closed his eyes and leaned his face against his fist.

"Quinn . . . why? What does she have to gain?"

"A bestselling book, a movie . . ."

"It's not about money. I've offered them money any number of times. She's always refused it."

". . . the adoration of thousands, maybe millions, the heartfelt sympathy, the love, the *attention*. Everything she's wanted all her life and was denied. Even you called her a saint, and if you haven't fallen in love with her yet it's because she already has an imaginary husband and you have an imaginary wife."

"My wife isn't imaginary."

"Wrong word. My bad. Celeste's husband is, though, and so is her adopted son. They live in her head."

I caught my reflection on the mirrored wall. This wasn't a half-bad look for me. Lose another five pounds, I could pull off this look for spring. I thought, He should make a pass.

Instead, he sat down again and fell silent, hands folded between his legs, head drooping, sinking deep into himself. Lost and a little afraid. I felt sorry for him. Last time I had sex I was feeling sorry for someone. Do it again, I thought, and it'll start looking like a bad habit.

I don't know how long we sat like that, in silence, but at the end of it his head came up and without looking at me he took his checkbook and a Montblanc fountain pen out of his inside jacket pocket.

"Let's call it a full week," he said, and wrote out the check.

I waved it in the air, drying the ink, and said, "Thanks. I'd still like to get a voice analysis for you."

"I don't think so."

"Suit yourself. Me, I'd rather have the truth, however painful, than the lie, however pleasant. But that's me. I'm a realist."

"And yet you believe we pass from this life into another, as a living, breathing person."

"Or animal, if you screw up. Or off the wheel if you've nailed it."

We were done there, but neither one of us rose from the table and neither one of us felt like finishing the coffee going cold in front of us on the table.

"Alex," I said, "why exactly did you ferry over here and knock on my door this morning?"

"Danny's been thrown for a loop. Everything affects him physically. He's in the hospital right now."

I almost laughed at how he was able to ignore everything I had just told him. Almost.

He unfolded the morning *Times* and turned it toward me. He pointed to a picture on the lower right. A death mask photo of a woman. I quickly scanned the story. An unidentified woman, fifty to sixty years old, was found dead last night in the new sculpture park. She was naked, laid out on a black steel trapezoid. No clothes were found at the scene. They were asking the public's help in identifying her. The police had no leads and had not yet determined the cause of death. I looked up at him.

"Grim little story," I said.

He took out his microrecorder from his side pocket and pressed the PLAY button. He placed the recorder in the center of the table, and we listened to it together.

Krapp's Cassette unnumbered (complete)

—(*Krapp*) Hello?
—Alex, it's Celeste. (*Whimpering, strange crying sound in b.g.*)
—What's wrong, Celeste?
—Danny's in trouble; we're going to have to take him to the hospital.
—What happened?
—His lungs are filling and he's spiked a fever. And the poor little guy is trembling. It's like . . . I don't know what it's like. It's my fault, I called it wrong.
—What?
—Do you have the morning paper?
—Yeah, right here.
—Do you see the picture of that woman who was found dead?
(*Brief pause*)
—Yeah, I've got it.
—It's Danny's birth mother.

—*What!*

—*I recognized her as soon as I saw the picture. Vic told me not to tell him, but I thought it would be a relief. She's the thing that's been haunting his dreams, the fear he's had to live with. But everything that happens is a risk to his health. I was as calm as I could be, but . . . Wait a minute.*

—*(Vic's voice in b.g) I'm gonna have to take you to the hospital, buddy. There's more going on here than I can handle.*

—*(Whispers) He looks bad, Alex. I could just kick myself.*

—*I would have done the same thing, Celeste. He has a right to know.*

—*I sat down with him and as calmly as I could I told him that finally a justice had been done. He asked me what and I told him the incubator—that's how he used to refer to her—*

—*I know, her and the sperm donor.*

—*Right. These were the people who almost killed him and made his life a living hell. Anyway, I told him she was dead, and at first he did seem relieved. He let out a long breath. His shoulders shook and then seemed to melt. He asked me how and I gave him the newspaper. He read the story and within half an hour he was spiraling.*

—*God . . .*

—*I didn't realize how scary these people really are to him. I should have. God, that's why I've been keeping him so well-hidden. He knew right away what the story doesn't tell. That woman was murdered by the cult she was part of.*

—*Satanists? How does he know?*

—*He knows. It was a ritualistic murder. I think that after*

Danny escaped and the father was arrested, word got to
her and she never went back. She went off on her own
and somehow the group saw her as a threat. I don't
know, but it brought back some memories Danny
couldn't handle.

—Is there anything I can do?

—As soon as he's able to talk, I'll call. You always give him
such a lift. But right now we have to get him to the
hospital.

—Which one?

—I don't know. Vic decides that. I have to go now.

—All right, Celeste. Tell him I love him.

—I will. Bye.

24

I PULLED ON A PAIR OF UGG BOOTS AND MY PARKA. HE didn't want me to, but I was going to walk him to the ferry. As much as I may have wanted to get off the case, I thought it was still unfinished, especially now.

In the elevator, I said, "When I talked to Eve Gosler last night and asked her why she was still in Seattle, since she spiked the story, she said she wanted to see the sculpture park."

"Really? Coincidence?"

"Not even that, probably. Anybody coming into town wants to see the park. Besides, it was just an excuse for staying in town. Vic is the reason she's still here."

"So?"

"So nothing, I guess, because I've been fired."

"You haven't been fired," he said, a little impatiently, "you did your job. It's over now."

"I wish I felt that way."

In the lobby, he tried to open the door for me. I pushed the button on the side and the door popped open.

"That woman wasn't killed in the sculpture park," I said. "She was killed somewhere else and dumped there."

"What makes you think so?"

"It's pretty obvious. And *dumped* is not the right word. She was posed there, like a piece of the art."

At the corner, we came into range of my three Indians, who waved enthusiastically and shouted out words of sexual encouragement. They thought I had spent the night with someone.

"Suffer," I called back to them. Let them believe what they wanted to. A small corner of me was pleased to know that anyone, even three winos, thought I was capable of romance.

"Do you know those people?" Krapp asked me.

"Yeah. They helped me finger a killer once. We're pals now."

"That case?"

"Yeah, that case. So I owe them. Sometimes I think life is all about who owes what to who."

"How do you pay off a debt like that?"

"Lately, with Pepsi and Marlboros. They'll probably all die before I'm square with them."

We crossed First Avenue and headed toward Coleman Dock and the ferry.

"You didn't come over here to fire me," I said. "You came over to see what I made of Danny's dead mother in the park."

"I guess. But that was before you told me about the reporter. I'm taking Eve Gosler at her word. I think HBO will, too."

"Never happen. The seed of doubt's been planted. They

probably won't even take *your* word at this point. They'll expect you've been co-opted."

"What *do* you make of that murder, Quinn?"

"It doesn't change anything, not as far as you're concerned."

"No, it doesn't. Once Danny gets over it."

We passed under the viaduct, the sound of traffic rumbling above our heads. They plan to tear down the viaduct before the next earthquake drops it and kills everybody on it and under it, like me and Alex, now. The debate is over how to replace it. I should care. We waited to cross Alaskan Way.

He got a little dreamy on me and said, "You think people ever truly appreciate the inestimable benefit of having a good father, a decent man who doesn't beat you or starve you or fuck you?"

"The ones who had a good father probably take it for granted."

"Why shouldn't they? Every little boy and girl deserves a loving father. I had one."

"So did I."

"Mine was a fair man, honest and generous, quietly proud of his children, though he did keep a tight lid on his emotions."

"They did that then. Clammed up emotionally. My old man never told me he loved me till he knew he was dying. But there was never a moment when I doubted he did."

The screenwriter nodded. "I tell Danny I love him every time I talk to him, and I can feel it across the phone lines—the lift it gives him, the fulfilled promise of his dream of one day finding a true father. There has to be a protective father, and a loving mother, out there, for everyone."

"It doesn't hurt to hope."

We crossed the street to the water side and walked toward the ferry landing.

"Back in the eighties," he said, "there were accusations against this preschool, against its teachers and its founders, in LA."

"The McMartin trials. I remember it well. I was there then."

"They were accusing them all of Satanic ritual abuse. Children told of witches flying through the air, of sex with giraffes, secret tunnels under the school, all kinds of horrors. The woman who made the first accusations, one of the mothers, was a paranoid-schizoid. She started the ball rolling and then the shrinks got at the kids. They interviewed the children and concluded that more than three hundred of them had been abused. Three hundred kids in one school. They arrested everybody in sight, without any physical evidence. The trials went on for six years. They finally dismissed the cases on the teachers, but by that time the public believed that some kind of Satanic abuse must have taken place."

"It was a bad time, a kind of hysteria."

"The old lady who founded the school and her son were held without bail. They were in jail for about five years before they were acquitted."

"It was wacky."

"The school was closed and razed and the whole area was doused with holy water."

"What's more scary than Satan?"

"Exactly."

"Back then," I confessed, "I kind of believed they did it."

"So did I. I'm a little ashamed to admit it."

"Me too."

"Quinn, do you think that dead woman was a Satanist?

Danny said she was. Do you think she was killed by other Satanists?"

"You want me to find out? That's what I do for a living."

"No. I've got an eighty-million-dollar movie to rescue." He smiled. "That's what *I* do for a living."

We were at the entrance to the ferry station. I wasn't going up the ramp with him.

"Hold up," I said. "Here's where we say good-bye."

We had an awkward moment. I didn't know whether to thank him or rag him, kiss him or kick his ass. He didn't know whether to hug me or high-five me, dip me or ditch me.

Finally, he said, "Look, I'm not sentimental . . ."

"Neither am I."

". . . but at the end of the day, the only thing that matters is love."

"I've heard that said. Sung, even."

"And that Danny lives a little longer. That's all that's important to me."

I stared at him. I made myself cold and hard.

"Alex, there is no Danny. There's only Celeste pretending to be Danny. Save yourself."

He looked back at me, neither nodding nor shaking his head. Without another word, he turned and walked up the ramp. I watched him go, wondering if he might hesitate at the top, just to see if I was still watching, and if he'd smile.

He did, both things, though one of them a little wanly.

That was the last I ever saw of Alex Krapp.

25

I WANTED TO CLEAN MY APARTMENT AND TAKE THE WEEKEND off. Monday I could prep my tax stuff for L.H., my accountant. I could quietly sit in my office with a latte and wait for the phone to ring. I could go on to the next thing. But my gut was telling me to take it a click further before I could in good conscience drop this case into the "done that" file. It was also telling me I was hungry.

McDonald's was right there where I was standing watching the screenwriter go catch his ferry, but I have a grudge against the joint, so I went up the street to the Frankfurter. I wasn't going to eat one but I bought three with everything. (What did the Buddhist say to the hot dog vendor? Make me one with everything.) I doubled back and dropped the tube steaks on my Indians, cutting them off at, "She shoots, she scores." I went into the side entrance to the Pioneer Building.

I picked up two of Krapp's cassettes and put them into my purse. Alex never asked for the return of the cassettes he had given me. Considering that he had all of them cata-logued, it struck me as odd. I'd send them to his office. Even-tually.

I called Sergeant Beckman and talked him into meeting me for an early lunch at Serious Pie.

I took the number fifteen bus up to Pine Street, then walked over to Tom Douglas's new pizza joint on Virginia Street. On the way, I stopped at a vending box to buy the *Times*.

Beckman was already there, sitting alone at one of the tall community tables. I sat opposite him, taking off my parka and hanging it over the back of the chair. The heat from the wood ovens made the place nice and toasty. I ordered an onion-and-Gorgonzola pie. The sergeant went for pancetta and foraged mushrooms. We each ordered a Pabst Blue Rib-bon.

I slid the *Times* over to him and tapped on the story of the dead woman in the park.

"What?" he said.

"I might be able to help you with this."

"I'm all ears."

"I noticed that, but you got a big face, so it all hangs to-gether okay."

"I'm tired, Quinn. I've been up half the night. What have you got?"

"I can help you get an ID on the dead lady."

"We got an ID."

"Really?"

"She worked at the Safeway in Northgate, in the kitchen. One of her coworkers called it in. We're looking for next of kin."

"I can help you with that."

"Oh?"

"I know her son. Kind of."

"You got a name and address?"

"Again, kind of."

I told him the whole story, starting with my going down to LA to see Alex Krapp, noted screenwriter, then tailing Celeste and Vic, and talking to Eve Gosler. I told him why I wanted to see the governor last night. I told him about my client sticking a fork in me but me feeling a little underdone. Since Beckman had already checked out some of the history for me, he was pretty quickly brought up to speed.

By that time our pies arrived.

"So you know the next of kin, but the next of kin is an imaginary boy?" he said, around a mouthful of pizza. "Is that what you're telling me, Quinn?"

"I guess I am. I guess I'm not helping one bit."

"I guess you're not."

"How's your lunch?"

"Let's back up. A dead woman is found in the sculpture park . . ."

"Everybody shows up dead somewhere, eventually," I observed.

". . . naked, no clothes around, no weapon, no prints or DNA . . ."

"No nuttin'."

". . . laid out nice and orderly."

"You could almost say ritually."

I had his interest.

"Go on," he said.

"But she wasn't killed there."

"Won't know that till the ME makes his report. Right now, that's the crime scene, which is a bummer for the museum."

"She wasn't killed there," I repeated.

"Okay."

"There were no marks on the body? No signs of struggle?"

"Nope."

"Any sexual assault?"

"A little."

"Beckman . . . what's a little sexual assault?"

"Look, the press doesn't know about this."

"I have some failings. Talking to the press is not one of them. You know that."

"Yeah."

I gave him a moment.

He said, "A communion wafer was wedged up in her vagina."

"Woi Yesus," I said flatly.

"We're looking for a priest."

"Or some pious lunatic who drank the Blood but palmed the Body for later."

"Your Satanist angle?"

"Let's not go too gently into that night."

"Truth is, nobody would mind a little help on this, you got anything?"

"For you, free of charge. Although I could use a favor."

"Like every time I see you. Apropos, I got a name for you." He took out his notebook. "The black Ford Explorer belongs to a Glen Yukilis."

"You're kidding."

"You know him?"

"Yukilis? Of course I don't know him. Who the hell is he?"

"I got an address."

He gave me a number on Northeast Sixty-ninth Street. I wrote it into my notebook.

"So that's one more favor. You've reached your weekly quota," he said.

"Am I being intrusive? Am I putting you out? Am I putting you at risk of losing your money or your job or your good name?"

"All right, all right, what the hell do you want?"

I slid the two cassettes across the table.

"There's a woman and a boy on these tapes. The boy's about fifteen, but still prepubescent."

"Your imaginary son of the dead woman?"

"Yeah."

"And your other imaginary mother."

"That one's for real. I want your voice analyst to listen to both voices and tell me who's who."

"Who's who?"

"Are the woman's voice and the boy's voice the same voice? That's what I need to know, to get a good night's sleep."

"That's a budget item, Quinn."

"Charge it to the dead lady in the park."

He let out the sigh of a put-upon cop. You can recognize it when you hear it. Hell, I invented it.

"Good man," I said. "Put a rush on it. Lunch is on me."

He put the cassettes into his pocket and stepped down from his chair.

"By the way," I said. "You ID'd the woman, you said. So what's her name?"

He told me, then spelled it out. He didn't have to.

"Jeez, Quinn, you've gone all pale. Was it the Gorgonzola?"

26

Did I say I was going to clean my apartment and take the rest of the weekend off?

The last thing I wanted to do that cold Saturday was drive to Walla Walla, a miserable drive under the best of circumstances, and these were not the best of circumstances. It was snowing on Snoqualmie Pass, and here's my little PT chugging up the mountain without chains. Holding my breath got me over the summit and down below the snow line, but then I was worried about getting back. Please, God, don't make me have to spend the night in Ellensburg.

Safely on the other side of the mountain, I felt inclined to answer my ringing phone. It was Beckman. The reception wasn't all that bad.

"You were right," he said. "Next of kin is a cop, or used to be."

"You doubted me?"

"Oh, no, never, only sometimes I'm not so sure."

"Any reaction?"

"I don't know. I wasn't the one notifying, and obviously the guy isn't a suspect, since he's already at McNeil Island."

"Could be the contractor."

"Don't make this any more complicated than it is."

"Just because you're in prison doesn't mean you can't get a person whacked somewhere else. It happens."

"All right, we'll see how that pans out. Listen, Quinn, it's gonna be in the papers. Odds are, your name's gonna come up, because of the old case."

"That's okay, but do you think you can hold the press off on that until you hear from the ME?"

"Right now it's a novelty murder so they're camping out on my doorstep, but I'll do my best."

"Thanks, amigo."

I struggled to stay awake. I kept asking myself why I was doing this, but that only served to make me sleepier. And the reward at the end of my journey: Walla Walla State Prison.

Not to bad-mouth Walla Walla. Used to be just mighty fine onions, but now they've got wine tasting rooms. Without the prison, it's kind of a nice little town. A hundred years ago the locals had the choice of having a prison or a state university built in their town. They took the prison; saw more future in it.

I stopped at a Jiffy Mart and bought a carton of Camels and a liter of cold Fresca. Once past the gate, I was shown to the warden's office. We made the usual joke about meeting this way, and then he asked for my weapon. I gave him my whole purse: the LadySmith, the Mentos, and the Ogens, taking with me only the cigarettes, the Fresca, and the *Times*. He led me to a chilly gray room where no one's ever had a genuine laugh.

"I'm going to have to put a guard in here with you," the warden said.

"Please," said I.

I sat alone in one of four institutional chairs for about ten minutes.

The door opened and Randy Merck came in, a guard behind him with pecs you could tap-dance on.

"Quinn," Randy said, like I was his long-lost favorite aunt.

He opened his arms wide for a hug. Not in this lifetime, nor the next. Nor the one after that. I bumped fists with him. He thought I was a dyke anyway. Suffer.

"Sit down, Randy."

"Don't mind if I do. How're you doin', Quinn?"

"Here, I got you something." I picked up the bag from the floor and gave it to him. I looked at the guard and said, "I cleared it with the warden." I left the newspaper on the floor.

The guard nodded.

Randy twisted off the cap and sucked down more Fresca than I would care to drink in an entire afternoon. In an entire lifetime.

"I remember you had a jones for cold soft drinks," I said.

"Yeah, but you never knew why. Thanks, Quinn."

He broke open the carton of cigarettes and turned around to look at the guard. The guard nodded again. Randy lit up and luxuriated: smoke and soda. I wondered what he meant: *never knew why.*

"Still chasin' the devil?" he asked.

"In a way."

"Do as thou wilt."

"Huh?" I said. The words came out of his mouth but seemed to be coming from beyond.

"It's their motto. In other words, anything goes. All the stuff the dweebs say you shouldn't do, the Satanists say, knock yourself out. Rape, steal, kill. It's all there for your enjoyment."

"Including abusing children."

"Especially abusing children. Top of the list. Killing a kid is the big bingo. That's the greatest release of magic energy. You're the baddest then."

"And you were into it?"

"Had to be, as a kid. It was how I stayed alive. Okay, I wound up a little twisted, but I ain't touched any of that shit since I made my escape."

"When was that?"

"When I was thirteen. That's when I went into the system, which was a relief, frankly. I never felt so looked after."

I remembered how he got into the system at age thirteen. Rape.

"Okay, so what is the reason you swill soda?"

"A kid raised with them, you never get the taste out of your mouth. Chewing gum, LifeSavers, cold soda. Nothing gets rid of it."

"Jesus, Randy . . ."

"You name it, it's been there. Hey, cheer up, I've made an adequate social adjustment. They told me so, in here. I don't have to act out anymore."

"You're bullshitting me, right?"

"About what?"

"About adjusting."

"To tell you the truth, I don't even know. Shit, it's possible.

I could get out of here, square up, and get a good job painting people's houses. Or not."

I didn't know whether to punch out his lights or pat him on the back.

"You're a vegetarian, aren't you, Randy?"

"Yeah."

"Is that part of it?"

"Oh, no, they're all carnivores. They'll eat it on the hoof. But when you're force-fed raw meat as a tyke, well, you know, once you can choose for yourself, you're gonna choose something that doesn't bleed."

"Are you afraid of them? Still?"

"Not really. I stay away from them. They got no interest in me. What are you working on, Quinn?"

"Now? Just curiosity. And maybe a murder case."

"Satanists? Wow. They never leave no evidence. They got it down to an art and a science. Hey, let me help you, like I did before."

"Before? You did nothing but fuck it up."

"I'm hurt."

"Suffer."

"Tell me who got murdered. C'mon, you didn't come here just to visit an old friend."

"I got no friends in here."

I picked up the *Times* from the floor and unfolded it. I handed it over to Randy.

He looked at the picture. His brow knitted, as though trying to place the lady, and then he got up. The guard didn't move forward but he seemed to grow an inch. Randy paced the room, nothing to see and nothing to do but walk it off in the box we were in.

"Wow," he mumbled. "Wow. Holy shit . . ."

"Sorry, kid, I'm sure it's a shock," I said.

"Yeah, they left a body. That's a jolt. What the hell are they saying? There's a message here, Quinn."

"Randy, it's your mother."

"Oh, yeah. Boo-hoo."

"I guess we all grieve in our own ways."

"Look to the old man, Quinn."

"Your father?"

"That son of a bitch engineered this. He's cold, man, the coldest."

"I thought it a possibility."

"Oh, yeah."

"What's it all mean, do you know? Naked, lying on a piece of sculpture."

"Black Mass, man, out to suck up some real juju."

"So the sculpture is what, an altar?"

"Fuck, no, *she's* the altar. Don't be surprised if a real priest officiated. Some of them have gone to the dark side. It's all about fucking, one way or the other. The priests all swore off of it, so the fuckers can't think of anything else. Along comes a Satanist and says, Help yourself. Do as thou wilt. The priests know the lingo, so they just twist it upside down and do the true nasty. You talk about being scared? This is scary. Put the heat on the old man, look for a fallen priest."

"You didn't like her one bit, did you?"

"Please. She was an evil bitch and she got what she deserved. Tell me what you got."

"There wasn't a mark on her. Still don't know the cause of death."

"Hell, I know how she died."

"How?"

"Tell them to check her lungs. They'll be full of water. She drowneded."

"Drowned? And then taken there?"

"Quinn, you ever hear of trial by ordeal?"

"Yeah. Primitive tribes sometimes judge criminals by putting them through something, an ordeal."

"Like holding them underwater. If they don't drown, they're cool. If they do, they're guilty. And already punished 'cause they're dead."

He sat down again and pulled off his shoes and socks. He put one foot on his knee and showed me the sole. It was full of scar tissue, of a kind I'd seen before, up close, the kind left by fire.

"You've been through it? A trial by ordeal."

"They thought I told a teacher, you know, about what they were doing to me, which I didn't. I never would. Made me walk over hot coals. I passed."

My stomach was turning over that pizza I had for lunch. I wanted to reach for one of his cigarettes.

"There's something else, Randy. Maybe you can explain it."

"Shoot."

"There was a communion wafer wedged up inside her vagina."

He calmly put back on his sock and shoe.

"Well, that's a little different."

"I'd say so."

"No, not that they'd do that. But what happens is that once the priest puts it up in there, he fucks her. Then they line up and run a train on her. I don't know why they would put it there and not do the rest."

We sat for a few moments in silence. I'd really heard enough; I was played out. I started thinking about a hot bath and a long warm sleep. Maybe I'd get a room in Ellensburg and spend the night. I could hardly hold up my head.

"Sorry for your loss," I said.

He made a goofy face. My nerves were about to shake out through the top of my head.

"Randy, did you have any siblings?"

"I had a little brother. It went harder on him, 'cause he fought against it. I don't know what ever happened to him."

I showed him my picture of Danny.

"Where'd you get this?"

"A client gave it to me. You know him?"

"It's my little brother, Victor."

On the way back to the car, I had a hot flash so bad my nose started bleeding. I stuffed it with Kleenex and drove away.

27

IT WAS DARK DRIVING BACK, AND I WAS EXHAUSTED. THE visit reminded me of the last time I dealt with Randy. He wore me out then, too. I cracked a window and sucked some frigid air into my wide-open mouth. I actually considered getting a room in Ellensburg, but I could never take a bath in a motel room.

I pressed on, up the mountain. I'd called the highway patrol and found out the roads were clear. I fumbled with my phone and put in a call to Beckman. I had to leave a message.

He called me back when I was rolling down into Issaquah, just a half hour out of Seattle.

"You sitting down?" I asked him.

"Yeah, with my feet up and a stiff drink in my hand. You sound a little funny, Quinn."

"Hold on."

I pulled the clotted Kleenex out of my nostrils.

"Okay. I'm glad you're sitting down, because this is gonna blow your mind."

"Haven't had a blow job in three months. Go."

"I saw the surviving son, Randy, and showed him the picture. Bereaved he was not, nor too surprised, either. He thinks his old man engineered it, too, carried out by Satanists. I'll save you the details 'cause I don't want you spitting out your drink, but he says it was a Black Mass. Your lady drowned, dunked underwater in a trial by ordeal. For what? Who knows? Probably for hiding out and working at the Safeway."

I waited for him to sputter something, but I got dead air.

"I told you it would blow your mind."

"Quinn?"

"Yeah?"

"You are so full of shit."

"Just call the ME and have him check her lungs."

"He already has. And her bloodstream and her stomach and all her orifices. There was no water or anything else in her lungs. But in her stomach, some Seconals and a poison that's being analyzed as we speak. Exposure a contributing factor. So it's looking more like she was alive when she was laid out in the park. Stay tuned. Drive carefully, De*tec*tive."

He put that sarcastic spin on the second syllable and hung up on me.

I hit the hazard blinkers and pulled to the side of the road. Traffic whizzed by at a hundred per while I hammered the steering wheel, shouted shit to the overhead, and hurt my big toe kicking the dashboard.

That puny prick punk puke twisted rapist serial assaulter dyed-in-the-wool fucking liar Fresca-sucking son of a bitch jailbird Randy! He got me again. He rolled out the bullshit slide and I took a running belly flop. I knew some of it had to be real, but that's the way it is with sociopathic shitferbrains attention-seeking perverted excuses for human beings. You never know which parts of their convoluted fantasies are true. I knew he had fragments of needles and pins in his scrotum; I saw the X-rays. And I knew his father tortured him. Or did I? Did I know any more about Randy than Alex knew about Danny? Like, Alex didn't even know the kid in the picture was named Victor and was . . . da frick! How did I even know that *that* was true? Raised by devils, Randy was diabolical. He saw the picture and had a quick thought: let's mess her up even more. Son of a bitch! I kicked out with my good toe. Still, though, I thought, when I calmed down. How could he come up with the name *Victor*?

Back in my apartment I opened up a can and microwaved a bowl of lentil soup while the bath filled with water as hot as I could stand it. I stood at the window in my bathrobe and ate the soup, looking down at the pergola. The streets were crowded with young revelers, and even with the doors to the bars shut I could hear three different bands, each as bad as the other. My Indians were beating on cardboard boxes and chanting, drawing a pretty good crowd of drunk kids, the tribal spirit moving them.

I rinsed out the bowl and left it in the sink. I took the bottle of Stoli out of the freezer and poured three fingers of the icy vodka into a plastic glass. In the bathroom, I hung up my robe and stepped into the bath. I slid down into the scalding water and sipped my drink, trying to wash away the whole day, inside and out. Icy cold in, scalding hot out.

The water eventually cooled, which might have been what woke me up. I couldn't say how long I'd been sleeping but the streets were quiet, so it had to have been hours. I didn't want to wake up. I thought of turning on the hot water with my foot and falling back into that peaceful darkness, but I didn't want to wind up as the lady who *did* drown.

I opened the drain and lay there for another few minutes before getting out of the tub and drying off. Fully awake now, it landed back on me how much of an amateur I must have sounded like to Beckman. I made up my mind to lose Randy Merck like lint. Still, even if it wasn't trial by ordeal, that lady had to have been the star in a dark ritual. A naked woman, laid out on what could only be considered an altar, like a sacrifice, with a communion wafer up in her stuff? Who does that, if not Satanists or some other kind of twisted cult?

Nude, I walked out to my living room, startling myself still again on the mirrored wall. Would I ever get used to it? I didn't look half bad, really. I looked back at the kitchen clock. Two-thirty. Outside the streets were all but deserted, just the occasional prowling insomniac or odd-hours worker. Even my Indians were tucked into their sleeping bags, way down inside them. It looked cold out. How long would a naked woman last on a night like this?

Some things just come to you, standing without any clothes on and looking out the window. I was dying for some more sleep and the comfort of my own bed, the warmth of my own little nest, but I knew that wasn't going to happen. Less than twenty-four hours had passed since they'd found Randy's mother. Maybe there was still time to redeem myself.

I bundled up, stuffed my LadySmith into the right pocket of my parka and my wallet in the other pocket, and went down to the parking garage. I fired up the PT and ran up Western Avenue, behind the deserted Public Market, to the sculpture park. I parked inside the Old Spaghetti Factory lot and did a slow walk around the park.

I looked at the cars and I looked at the curbs. It wasn't long before I found a crushed can. I stooped down to examine it. There was a stain all around it, so it had been run over still containing most of its contents, which was Drano, the stuff you use to unclog a drain. I stuck my pencil in the top and set it down on the sidewalk. I walked on.

Most cars you can squeeze the handle and not set off an alarm; others, all you have to do is cough and they will start howling, not that anyone pays any attention to that anymore. The car alarm has become one of modern times' most useless, if not most annoying, inventions. I had no worries about being busted as a car prowler, but I did not want to wake up the whole neighborhood. I checked the several cars still left on the street, eliminating the high-end and even the mid-range. I was looking for a beater. And I found it, a rusted-out Honda Civic that looked like it had half a million miles on it.

I aimed my powerful mini–power light through the passenger-side window and saw that the keys were in the ignition. Neatly stacked on the passenger seat were her clothes, shoes on top. I tried the door. It was unlocked. I opened it and quietly shut it again.

Already nodding on Seconals, the wretch of a woman must have stripped in her car and stepped out naked to the deserted street, into a temperature around twenty-two degrees. She walked toward the park, chugging enough Drano to unclog everything, then tossed the can. Unseen and undetected in the cold middle of the night, she entered the sculpture park, climbed onto the black steel slab, and put her poisoned body and tortured mind to sleep. Oh, that other thing. Lying there, she opened her cold palm and, for reasons only she could know, inserted the Body of Christ into the doorway of life.

I called Beckman at home. He answered on the first ring.

"Don't you ever sleep?" I asked.

"Used to. I've lost the knack."

"It doesn't have to be you, but somebody should come down to the sculpture park. I'm here next to an oxidized Honda Civic. Your dead lady's clothes are folded and stacked inside. Key's in the ignition. The poison she used was Drano, which beyond the symbolism has got to be one wicked cocktail. The can will have her prints on it. I can't say the Satanists are without blame, but nobody laid her out on that steel slab. This was a one-woman show."

"I'm on my way."

28

I WENT BACK TO MY CAR, NOT SURE I WANTED TO WAIT FOR Beckman or go home. There was nothing more I could do besides suck up a little validation, which most of the time is worth the wait. I was exhausted, though, and longing for my warm bed.

As I pulled out onto Broad Street, I saw the taillights of the black Ford Explorer go up the hill and turn right onto First Avenue. My warm bed would still be there. I had to get to the bottom of why someone named Glen Yukilis was haunting me.

I followed him down First to Battery, then left to Denny Way, where he took a right, which worried me because he could have gone straight up Broad and taken a right on Denny. I was afraid he was on to me. There was very little traffic besides us two. I dropped back a bit but kept him in sight.

He made a left on Twelfth Avenue and sped up, making a fast right on East Aloha and another left on Fifteenth. He pulled to the curb. A block away, I did likewise, cutting the lights. He ran across the street toward Volunteer Park. I pulled out again and tried to run him down, but he jumped into the Lake View Cemetery.

I left my car and took off after him on foot.

He was dressed in black and hard to see in the moonless night.

Once inside the cemetery, I lost him. Standing alone in a cemetery in the middle of the night primes the adrenaline pump. I was alone among the headstones and had the unsettling feeling that I might have been lured into a trap, like I might have just offered myself up as the guest of honor at a real Black Mass.

I'd just decided to retrace my steps and stake out his car when a nervous voice sounded from behind a tree: "I've got a gun."

I dove behind a headstone and shouted out, "So do I!"

I took the LadySmith out of my parka pocket and pointed it in his general direction. Frozen flowers were on the grave I was intruding upon, lots of them, and bits and pieces of other stuff: cards, drawings, a small bottle of something. I took out my mini-light and flashed it on the headstone. I was lying atop Bruce Lee, taking cover behind his headstone. His son Brandon was buried next to him, and the mementos left by fans spilled over both graves.

From behind the tree the yonko yelled, "Who the hell are you?"

"You first. Why are you following me?"

"You're following *me*, bitch."

"Before that. And watch your mouth, asshole."

"Quinn?"

"Yeah?"

"All right, I have been tailing you. I'm a PI."

"So am I."

"I know that."

"What's your name?"

"Moss. Pete Moss."

I fired a shot into the air. It landed I know not where.

"The fuck!" was his response.

I put in a quick call to Beckman, on his cell. I figured he was on his way to the sculpture park, if not already there.

"Where you at?" I said, when he answered.

"On the way."

"I need you to make a detour. Shots have been fired. Well, a shot."

"Where?"

"Lake View Cemetery. On the grave of Bruce Lee."

"Quinn?"

"I'm serious."

"Why didn't you call nine-one-one?"

" 'Cause they tape those calls and I don't want the tape played in court after I kill this yonko. I don't want the DA saying there wasn't enough emotion in my voice."

"There's enough emotion in your voice," said my favorite cop.

"Get over here, please. Bring the cavalry."

"Who's shooting at you?"

"Nobody yet. I'm shooting at him."

"Who?"

"The yonko who's been following me." I yelled at the man behind the tree, keeping Beckman on the line. "You're Glen Yukilis, asshole."

"That's my real name. Pete Moss is my professional name. Don't you have a professional name?"

I thought for a moment. Damn, it does make sense to have a different name for business. I was far too visible and open for the line of work I found myself in.

"Quinn?" From Beckman.

"Hold on," I told him, then yelled to the other guy, "Why are you tailing me?"

"I won't anymore."

"Not if I kill you."

"Even if you don't."

"So why were you in the first place?"

"Your ex hired me."

My first impulse was to fire off another round. I ate the urge.

"What's his name?"

"Who?"

"My ex."

"Connors, from Spokane."

"What's he do for a living?"

"He's a pharmacist."

I spoke into the telephone. "Forget about it, Beckman. This situation's going to be handled by a short and unpleasant and, though I will try to control myself, angry phone call. As you were."

I hung up and shouted out, "Da frick!"

"Huh? What?"

"Why for?"

"Why for what?" he said.

"What did he want, my ex?"

"He wants to know what you're doing."

I put the gun back into my pocket and stood up. I walked toward his tree.

"All right, come on out. And put away your gun."

"Put away yours."

"I already have."

"You fired it."

"Not at you. I was frustrated."

"Well, jeez. What if everybody fired off a shot whenever they got frustrated?"

Tentatively, he stepped from behind the tree. It was the same dude I'd seen outside Celeste's house, the same one who'd boarded the bus with me.

"Why does he want to know what I'm doing? We're divorced, da frick."

"I could see you weren't together."

"So why did he want you to build a file on me?"

"Like I said, he wants to know what you're up to."

"What am I up to?"

"Nothing much. Working, it looks like. And there's a new man in your life. Lives on Bainbridge Island. Don't know his name."

"Would you say that man is handsome?"

"I guess so. Looks like he's got some money, too."

"So you'd say he's handsome and rich?"

"Yeah, I guess so."

"Would you say he's tall?"

"Six-one, six-two, yeah."

"Would you say he's dark?"

"No, I'd say he was fair."

"All right. So you'd say he was tall, fair, handsome, and rich?"

"Yeah, that's a pretty good description."

"Have you made your report for your client?"

"Not yet."

"Make your report. Tomorrow. And then quit. Because I see you again, one of us is gonna die."

We walked together out of the cemetery. I was glad for the company—it was scary in there. He got into his car, I got into mine. I wasn't going to have to make that angry telephone call to Connors. Pete Moss's report would be enough.

29

THE CHECK CLEARED. ALEX WAS BACK IN LA AND OUT OF MY life, though it seemed he had hardly ever been in it. I was back to waiting for the phone to ring, and if it had I might not have blown a day tracking down J. Gilbert Boum to a well-kept little house near the tip of Alki Point, where he lived with his wife of sixty years, who insisted I have a cup of green tea and a Jo-Jo. She used to bake, she told me, but these days takes the easy way out and buys her cookies at Trader Joe's. I high-fived her. My head hasn't been in an oven since that time I thought I might leave it there.

The retired professor wore a heavy knit cardigan and a pair of glasses on his high forehead. We sat in the "sun room," sans sun.

I'd got his name from Seattle Community College, where he put in thirty years teaching English composition and creative writing. Records showed Celeste was one of his students. There were other teachers as well, in psychology and counseling, speech, and drama, but I was interested in this old boy because he'd been her creative writing teacher for two years running. I showed him her student ID picture.

"Oh, yes, I remember Celeste."

"Tell me what you remember about her."

"Well, she was a pleasant girl, though lonely, I thought. I never saw her with any friends. She was a mediocre writer at best, but she worked hard. She wrote fantasies, as I recall. Not my cup of tea."

"What kind of fantasies?"

"I can't remember the details. Silly stuff, really. The stories were rather dreamlike, often with anthropomorphic animals showing humans the power of love. I'm surprised I remember that much. Maybe her stuff was better than I thought."

"She took your class twice."

"Yes, that was allowed, though not for double credit. She really thought that she could become a professional writer. Why are you interested in poor Celeste?"

" 'Poor' Celeste?"

"Well, she's dead, isn't she?"

"What makes you think so?"

"She dropped out just before the end of the term. She told me she had terminal cancer and had only months to live, so she wasn't going to waste what time she had left in junior college. I can't say I blamed her. I was struck with sorrow for her—so young, just beginning her life. She looked healthy enough. She certainly hadn't lost any weight."

"And you never saw her or heard of her again?"

"No, not until now. You mean, she's not dead?"

Back in my office, I got a call from Beckman. He patched

me into the voice analyst who'd done the work on my cassettes. Why am I doing this? I asked myself. What more did I have to prove?

"It's a ninety-eight-percent certainty that the two voices are the same," the expert told me. "The woman is impersonating the boy."

"What's the other two percent?" I asked.

"It's peculiar. Somewhere in the mix there is a child's voice."

"How can that be?"

"I really can't say for sure. It's quite odd. I could do a much more in-depth analysis, but I was asked just to ascertain if the two voices were the same."

"And you're sure in your mind that they are?"

"I'm sure. Ninety-eight percent sure."

I called Alex Krapp's office and got Gwendolyn.

"I haven't heard from him in days, Quinn. I'm getting a little worried. He usually checks in with me, even if he doesn't come into the office."

"When you hear from him, ask him, please, to call me. I have some new info for him."

I caught up on some filing and tried to organize my tax records, casting occasional glances at my two phones and hoping one of them would ring.

I finished my deskwork and leaned back in my chair. I thought about writing up a detailed report for Alex Krapp, but since he'd already fired me, I didn't see the point in wasting any more time than I already had. Still, I wanted him to know. I wanted him to call.

A tentative tap on the door brought me back.

"Come in."

Clifford Everybodytalksabout stuck his head inside my

office, like one not used to being indoors, and I might have been a little less than welcoming.

"What the hell are you doing in here, Clifford?"

He held aloft a small padded envelope. "An old dude on a Harley Road King gave us ten bucks each to give you this."

"When?"

"Just now."

I rushed to my window and looked down at the pergola. From my apartment I had the front view, from my office the back view. No Harley, no Indians. My plastic snake, Stanley, rested on the window ledge, scaring away pigeons. I turned back to Clifford, who was still peeking in from the hall.

"Get in here," I said.

He took small steps into the office and gently laid the envelope on my desk.

"What did he say, and I mean *exactly*?"

"He went, You know Quinn, the detective? And we went, Who wants to know? We're very protective of you."

"Yeah. Thanks. What else did he say?"

"He took that envelope from inside of his leather jacket. There was three tens clipped to it. He went, There's ten for each of you, if you deliver it to her. We were all over it. Nobody said nothin' after that."

"That was the whole conversation?"

"Word for word."

"Where are your two buddies?"

"Already spendin' the money."

I gave him another ten. He snatched it and backed out, telling me I was all right.

I opened the envelope and shook it over my desk. A microcassette fell out.

Krapp's Last Cassette (complete)

—(Celeste) Hi, Alex.
—Hi. What's wrong?
—You've come to know me so well, haven't you?
—I can hear it in your voice. What's wrong?
—It's not something bad, Alex. It could be very good. You have to have faith in that, faith in Danny. It could be the breakthrough we've been praying for.
—That's wonderful. What?
—There's a doctor in Paris who's been developing a protocol for cases like Danny. It involves a very intense hormonal therapy treatment, with experiments of bone marrow transplantation and blood transfusions. Bob has been working hard on coordinating some way for this to happen.
—I haven't heard much about Bob for a while.
—Well, we've been having our troubles, but he's really stood up on this one. He has a super-sensitive assignment over there and they really need him, so he's been able

to convince the Army to transport Danny to the
American Hospital in Paris so that he can participate
in this French doctor's protocol, which isn't available
over here.

—The Army will do that?

—Between you and me, the Army is ordering it, but
Halliburton is doing it. They're going to do it in secret
and hide the details. They don't really have to account for
anything. So the Army will get them to fly Danny to Paris
in an ambulance plane, keep him in the hospital there for
as long as it takes, and then, God willing, fly him back
here in much better shape.

—Is there a danger here?

—There's always a risk, in every procedure. But Vic has
been researching it and he thinks it's our best shot.
There's even a chance . . . there's an outside chance
he can make it. Maybe he doesn't have to die from
this.

—God, that's such great news. Will you be going with
him?

—Of course. It will give Bob and me a chance to get
together, at least for a few days, even if just to end the
marriage without rancor.

—You're going to divorce Bob?

—I have to. He wasn't cut out for this.

—What's Vic going to do?

—He'll stay here. He deserves some time off, and, frankly, I
worry about him. His own health isn't good. He really
needs a rest.

—Celeste, please, let me go with you, on the plane, just
for the plane ride there—I'll fly back on my own. I could
do whatever you have to do and take the flight. It

would mean the world to me. I'm sure it would help Danny.

—*Alex, you know if it were up to me . . .*

—*Who's it up to?*

—*The doctors, ultimately. And then there's Halliburton. They want to involve as few people as possible. And then there are still those . . . those people, who are still looking for Danny, so I have to . . . Look, I'll fight for it. I'll do everything I can. It's a great idea, really. It would make it such a fun flight for Danny, instead of one more scary experience. You know, he's never flown.*

—*Is he scared?*

—*Yes, he tries to be brave, but this is such a major disruption of his life.*

—*Please, let me go with you.*

—*For you, I'll work on it. I'll do my best. I promise.*

—*When is this going to happen?*

—*Soon, but I don't know when. They said an ambulance will show up at the door and we have to be ready to go, just like that.*

—*Can I talk to him?*

—*Sure. Hold on. Danny, it's your poppa.*

—*(Danny) Hi, Poppa.*

—*I just heard the great news.*

—*Yeah.*

—*You're a lucky boy.*

—*I know.*

—*You don't sound too happy about it.*

—*I'll be living in a hospital. Nobody knows for how long. It could be a long time. A long stretch in the Big House.*

—But you'll be getting better. You'll get your growth going. You can beat this.

—I won't be able to talk to you every day like we have been. I may not be able to talk to you at all.

—I'm going to get you a laptop. Load up a program called Skype. We can talk via the computer till the cows come home, for free.

—That'd be great, but from what I hear I'm gonna be getting treatment twenty-four/seven. I don't know what kind of free time I'll have, and if I'll physically be able.

—We'll deal with it. One thing I know: we will always be together.

—Always. Forever and ever. I love you, Poppa.

—And I love you, kid. We'll find a way to talk every day. I don't know what I would do if I couldn't talk to you every day.

—Me too. Vic is here with a trayful of medicine. I gotta go, Poppa.

—Danny . . . if you ever loved me, now is the time. Let me see you face-to-face and say good-bye.

—I want that so much, Poppa. I'm gonna try to convince Mom. Please, fly up here to Seattle. We'll find a way.

—I'm already in Seattle.

—You are?

—I'm on Bainbridge Island.

—Really? What are you doing there?

—It's a long story. I could be there in an hour or so. Just give me the address.

—Wow, Poppa. You're so close. I can't believe it.

—And I'm coming to see you.

(*Sounds of Danny crying*)

—*Danny?*

—*I'm okay. I'm just so happy you're here. I'm going to talk to Mom. I'll ask her to call you. I can't wait to see you.*

(*End of conversation*)

—(*Alex Krapp*) *Hello, Quinn. Right after this conversation, Celeste called and gave me her address and asked me to come in two hours, because she had to make some preparations. By the time I got on a ferry and found their house, it was closer to three hours. Vic met me at the door and told me I'd missed them by forty minutes. An ambulance had picked them up, taken them to Boeing Field, and they were in the air to France. In all the rush and confusion no one thought about calling me. I was numb. Vic told me he was going to check himself into the hospital for some tests. I haven't heard anything from anyone for the past couple of days, so I'm sure they are in the French hospital and Danny is undergoing the new protocol. And Vic is getting some rest. I keep my fingers crossed. (Long pause) It's hard to tell you what that boy has brought to my life. My wife used to tell me she never heard me laugh so hard as when I was talking to Danny. She never heard me sing, until Danny. She never saw me cry, until that dying boy came into my life. I'd like to say "our" life, but my wife knew it was a relationship so strong that she could only be a spectator. I told her what you said, that Danny wasn't real, that he was imagined. She said, "An imaginary friend is still a friend." Danny has given me what no friend in Hollywood even knows how to give. I've worked over thirty years in films and I don't have a single friend I could trust with my heart the way I entrusted it to Danny. Someday, I truly believe, he will walk through the door and give me a big hug. What I don't know is where that door will be. Right now, as you listen to this, I'm on the Harley, and the biker's creed works for all of this: The journey is the destination.*

30

I CALLED ALEX KRAPP EVERY DAY FOR THE NEXT TWO WEEKS, at all the numbers I had for him. I called Gwendolyn and told her where to find his Porsche. It had been sitting in long-term parking at LAX, gathering dust. For those first two weeks, the police couldn't get too excited about a missing man on a Harley.

Alex's wife reported a phone call from him. He told her he was headed south and would stay with her for a few days. Ten days passed without word, and Alex never rolled onto her property in Santa Barbara.

It became a news story, in LA first and then wider. His face even got five seconds on *Extra,* which brought in a deluge of sightings, none of which were helpful in locating him.

A check on his credit cards showed gas and motel charges from Canada to the Olympic Peninsula, down the Oregon coast to Half Moon Bay, just south of San Francisco, where they stopped.

The weeks became months. The cold became less cold;

the rain became mist. Though they had nothing concrete, the police concluded he probably went off Route 1, which can be a treacherous road, especially at night or in the rain. He could have gone off the road and into the Pacific at dozens of spots between Half Moon Bay and Morro Bay.

One night Sergeant Beckman joined me at Brasa for happy hour and said, "The dude was too old to be tooling a Harley down U.S. One. I'd call it the same way. Going too fast, dark night, wet road, missed a hairpin turn and went over the side like a rocket. Splash."

"Maybe he had a breakdown somewhere."

"So? He'd call Triple A."

"Not the mechanical kind. He was way ripe for a come-apart. He'd devoted more than a year of his life to comforting a dying boy who never was. He had a lot invested in that."

"So where do you go when you come apart?"

"You slip down into the nowhere special, to put the pieces back together. Either there or France."

"Ooo-la-la," he said flatly, summing up all he knew about France. He ordered another Jack on the rocks. I had another Sapphire Blue. And I'm no good after two.

"Either way, here I am," I said.

Even I didn't know what I meant.

"Put it behind you, Quinn," was Beckman's advice.

"Put what behind me?" said I.

More of those months went by, the way they do, either fast or slow. The days got long, with those ten o'clock sunsets that we live for up here. We had a couple hot days, ninety-four, -five, and all the pale skin in the Northwest came out to get fried. I had to go to Costco and make a capital expenditure on a small fan for my office. I sat behind my desk and leaned my face into the fan. Lately, my hot flashes were puny reminders of what they used to be. I could walk them off without my usual dread of spontaneously combusting. Maybe I was turning a corner. I should have been happy.

I'd discovered a Japanese barley tea that I could drink by the gallon, iced, without any ill effects. I was enjoying a tall glass of that and the breeze on my face when the phone rang. The caller ID read, "Out of Area."

I picked it up and said, "This is Quinn."

The caller said he was a novelist named Frank Sólyom. He had a low, somewhat flat voice with a hint of both culture and alley, as though he had gone to a good private prep school but on a wrestling scholarship. He spelled his name for me, including the accent mark, and said, "I only recently discovered my name had an accent mark. I'm reclaiming it. I think it might be a good career move."

He let out a little self-conscious chuckle and might have expected one from me, but I wasn't finding things very funny in those days.

"I'm calling about Alex Krapp," he said.

Though I hadn't heard that name in months, not many days passed by without my thinking about him.

"What about him?"

"I'm writing a book about his life and work. It's going to be called *Krapp's Last Cassette*."

I've read just enough Beckett to make me miserable. I fed Sólyom into the Google maw.

As I did, I asked, "What kind of a name is that?"

"Hungarian."

"I knew a Hungarian once. He was always depressed."

"Ah. We are not a happy people. Though we sometimes smile, we never laugh."

Google let me know he had written eight novels but

hadn't published anything in over twenty-five years. He had some mileage on him, a lot of it in the desert, apparently. Any career move he hoped to make at this point was going to be a kick for the finish line.

"What can I do for you, Mr. Sólyom with an accent mark?"

"Your name has come up in my research into the disappearance of Alex Krapp. They had a memorial for him a week ago, at the Writers Guild Theatre."

"So his colleagues think he's dead."

"You think he's still alive?"

"I hope so. I wouldn't know."

"His wife wanted it, the memorial. Closure and all that. It was a nice affair. Matthew Modine, the actor, recited Krapp's favorite poem."

"Oh, yeah, what was that?"

For an odd second or two, I thought he was talking about somebody. I didn't realize he was reciting a poem.

" 'Márgarét, áre you gríeving/Over Goldengrove unleaving?/Leáves, like the things of man, you/With your fresh thoughts care for, can you?/Áh, ás the heart grows older/It will come to such sights colder' and so on and so on. It's a poem about mortality."

"I used to read a little poetry. That was then. None of that walking all alone on the beach stuff, though. None of that poor me stuff."

"No, this one was poor you stuff. Poor everybody."

"Sounds like a fun read."

"His agent spoke at the memorial, and a few writers praised his work. The talk on the floor was disbelief that at his age he would be off on a motorcycle."

"He wasn't that old."

"Some of the writers there thought he pulled a disappearing act, but much of that may have been a kind of transference. Seems they've all dreamt about disappearing. As screenwriters in a director's medium, they're already halfway there. Others went with the conventional wisdom: He must have gone off the road and sunk into the sea—it's happened often enough before—because he had a deal to do a postproduction narration at a hundred grand a week. Money aside, he had a reputation for reliability, so a lot of the writers there thought he would never vanish on his own before finishing a job. Anyway, I wanted to talk to you about him, if you don't mind."

"I knew the guy for about a week."

"But apparently a real connection was made."

"It was?"

"It's on a cassette. He thought you might be, well, interested in him."

"That's not the same as him being maybe interested in me." He didn't say anything, so I said, "Was he? Was there a cassette like that."

"There are so many of them. In any case, I understand you did some work for him."

"Who told you that?"

"His secretary and his wife."

"My kind of work is confidential. Sorry."

I really didn't know who this yonko was, despite who he said he was. He could have been a reporter or another PI.

"I wouldn't ask you to breach any confidentiality. I know you were working on the Danny Timpkins thing. I know that you believed the boy didn't exist."

I didn't say anything.

"Ms. Quinn?"

"Yeah, I'm still here."

"You weren't the only one who believed that. I got the impression from Krapp's wife that she, too, came to believe he was imaginary."

"Oh?"

"Not the secretary, though. Gwendolyn still believes in the boy. She still hears from him, from time to time."

"Is that right?"

"By e-mail, from France."

"He's still in France?"

"Well, no, not according to you. According to you he doesn't exist."

"I forgot."

"But according to the people who do believe in him, he is doing quite well with the experimental protocol. He'll never be entirely healthy, I hear, but he may live a good long life."

"Where are you hearing all this?"

"Vic D'Amato, the doctor who took care of him."

"You talked to Vic?"

"On the telephone."

"And Celeste?"

"Not yet. She is in France, with Danny."

"Okay."

"I understand you are in possession of several cassettes that belong to Mr. Krapp."

"Yeah."

"I wonder if I could have those."

"I'll send them to Krapp's office."

"Fox has reassigned the office, I'm afraid. To Steve Guttenberg, the actor."

"Where's Gwendolyn?"

"Back in the secretarial pool. You could send the cassettes to me."

"Sure. Give me an address."

He gave me an address in New York. My guess, a mail drop. I lost it.

"I'm basing a good part of my book on his cassettes," he said. "I have quite a few of them. I look forward to listening to yours."

"Sure."

"He was a bit compulsive about his cassettes, I understand."

"Was he?"

"From the short time you knew Alex Krapp, would you say he was obsessive, generally, or unbalanced or maybe just a little eccentric, just generally?"

"Generally, I would say, I don't know, generally."

"I seem to be making you unhappy."

"Don't blame yourself."

"Does it disturb you, to talk about Krapp?"

"Well, I don't know you."

"I understand."

"Your voice sounds familiar, a little. Have we ever met?"

"No, I doubt it. I've never met a private detective, and I'm from the East Coast."

"So am I, originally. Pennsylvania."

"I'm from upstate New York. Owego."

"Where they have all the snow, Oswego?"

"No, the other one. Owego. They have snow there, too."

"Look, Mr. . . ." I'd already forgotten how to say his name.

"Call me Frank."

"Look, Frank, like I said, I knew Alex for about a week. Long enough to know he was a good guy. He could have gone on writing his screenplays, a million dollars a clatter, kissing movie stars, eating at the Ivy. He didn't deserve to have his heart turned inside out like that, to go through the pain of being a substitute father to a dying boy that turned out to be a wide acre of lies and a swamp of craziness. On the other hand, he didn't seem to mind. He wanted it. He needed it. I wonder how much he needs it now. He was had in the worst way you can be had, right to the bottom of your heart. Nothing of what enriched Alex's life during that time was real. It was a cruel hoax."

"But was it? How can love be cruel?"

"That's most of what it is."

"I can't believe that. It would hurt too much."

"You get used to it."

"But can you live without it? Love?"

"Look, what happened to Alex wasn't love. It was manipulation, a sick ploy and a twisted game."

I don't know, five seconds, ten seconds went by. It seemed longer.

"They used to sing together," he said wistfully.

"Alex?"

The phone went dead.

31

I SAT IN MY CAR AND STUDIED CELESTE'S HOUSE. I THOUGHT it a sad little place, full of strange secrets, but how would I know? How would anyone know, about this house or any other? What is a house, from the outside, but sticks and stones? Inside, though, whole worlds are imagined into being.

I got out of the car, opened the gate, and went up to the front door. I rang the bell. In a moment it opened. I caught a glimpse of huge buttocks in a skirt too short retreating into the kitchen.

"Doctor D'Amato, I presume."

Vic stood with one hand still tight on the door edge, looking me over. "I've seen you before."

"At the TS Tavern. I'm Quinn. I'm the detective Alex Krapp once hired to prove that Danny Timpkins was a real boy."

"I always liked Alex."

"Then you're gonna be missing him because he's gone. Presumed dead."

"I heard."

"You ever hear of a writer name Frank Sólyom?"

"No."

"He never talked to you?"

"Never heard of him. So what are you doing here?"

"Here on my own. Let's talk."

"I'd rather not."

"I know the truth."

"Did it set you free?"

"What?"

"The truth is supposed to set you free."

"The honest person thinks so. Me, I wasn't all that tied up over it anyway. That was Alex and all the others who sunk their emotions into your sister's little creation."

"Danny is real," he said. "You want the truth? That's it."

"Yeah, I know. It took me awhile, on my own dime, but I finally found that out."

I caught him off-guard. He tried to cover his surprise.

"And you're here, why?"

"Invite me in, why don't you?"

"Because I don't know you and I don't much care about you."

"I could change that, with one phone call."

"Is that a threat?"

"Of course it's a threat."

"You can't do me any harm, and you sure can't do me any good."

"You never know, some good comes out of everything. But this I know for sure: I can do you some harm. Let's start with you practicing medicine without a license."

"You'd need a complaint."

"Hell, I'll complain, as a citizen. I've got cassettes. Alex taped all his conversations. You gave him medical advice. You gave medical advice to his friends: dosages, treatments, stuff like that. Even a school nurse isn't allowed to give you an aspirin."

He considered the possibilities for a moment. He could give me the boot and run the risk of having me haunt him, or he could talk to me now and get it over with. He let me in.

The living room seemed smaller than it actually was, shrinking inward from the edges, with a tiny brick fireplace and a short mantel covered with framed photos of Danny, of Danny and his best friend Perry, of Celeste and her "daughters."

Homemade shelves were jammed with books, mostly weathered paperbacks. The carpeting might have been orange once. The *Seattle Times* was spread on the easy chair, so I took the sofa. A pillow from a bed was at one end of it, suggesting somebody was accustomed to sleeping there.

"You might want to call in your sister," I said, "since she's the star player in Danny World."

"My sister?"

"Don't play dumb, Vic. I know Celeste is your sister."

"Celeste is out of the country."

"I saw her run out of the room when you opened the door."

"C'mon out, sis, the jig is up," he called, smiling.

The kitchen door opened, and since I was expecting to see Celeste, that's who I saw. Then I realized who it really was. I had to overcome the shock of seeing her. The blonde I'd seen in the tavern with Vic, the one with the great figure, had turned into, well, Celeste. She was obese now.

"Hello, Eve," I said.

She said nothing back.

"I gotta admit, this throws me, a little."

"I think I'll go do those errands now, Vic," she said.

"You know, don't you, that his name isn't Victor D'Amato? It's Eugene Volinsky."

She looked at me with dripping contempt.

"And you've either morphed or let yourself go, girl," I said. "This is not a good look for you."

Her eyes held nothing but contempt for me. They changed when she turned to Vic, who nodded.

She took her purse from the floor next to a bookcase, gave him a peck on the lips, and turned to me. "Good-bye," she said icily.

"See you around," said I. "Or not." After she left, I turned to Vic and said, "What the hell?"

He picked up the *Times* and sat on the easy chair. "Look," he said, "I don't have to answer any questions."

"No, you don't. You just have to listen. I came to unload."

He put one stockinged foot up on a hassock and left the prosthetic one on the floor.

"So unload."

32

I WAS SITTING A LITTLE TOO CLOSE TO VIC.

Let's call him Vic since that's what his girlfriend calls him. I walked the few steps to the fireplace and stood with my back to it.

"It happened just as Celeste said it did, in that book she wrote under Danny's name," I said. "A young boy who was suffering unspeakable abuse decided his only way to escape was to kill himself, but he saw the number for a hotline and he called. He got Celeste, a volunteer. Celeste was good on the phone. Phones were made for her. She could be anybody on a phone. The kid's name was not Danny. His name was Victor Merck, which is probably why Celeste changed your name to Victor. But I'll get to all that. First, Celeste's dream of becoming a writer. Maybe it all started with that, her need to be noticed for something good. Now, the book she wrote wasn't about her . . . Let me change that. *Everything* is about Celeste, but she chose to leave a lot out of the book, stuff about her, about how she had always been obese and unpopular, how she never had a boyfriend or a meaningful job or a circle of friends. Her one true talent was not writing; she's a mediocre writer at best. Her true talent is talking on the telephone. The only money she ever earned, before this book, was as a tele-marketer, one of those people who call you at dinnertime and you want to kill. Except for Celeste. The people she called cold wound up liking her, buying what she was selling, but she had scruples, at least when it came to money, and she felt bad about talking people into buying shit they didn't need. She'd rather have had their love. So she volunteered for a sui-cide hotline, and she was good at that, too. Waiting for calls, she imagined a service center, founded and managed by her: the Sunrise Service Center. She staffed it with people she imagined, including an older, handsome retired Army officer named Bob, who liked to flirt with her.

"Anyway, she gets a call from this poor desperate and sick kid. She arranges to meet with him, have some hot chocolate. Just like in the book. She takes him to the hospital, calls social services, promises the kid he'll never have to go back to that hell he was living in. That much was true.

"The kid was very sick and badly injured. They admitted him to the hospital. She stood vigil. She imagined herself waiting there with Bob, talking about this sad situation, talk-ing intimately about her dreams of changing the world through the power of love, and finally talking about adopting this boy and becoming his mother. She imagined Bob falling in love with her and wanting to adopt the boy with her. But none of that happened, did it? Because it couldn't. Because the real boy actually did die, didn't he?"

The face Vic had been wearing no longer held up. Some of him seemed to be puddling out. He reached down and pulled his prosthetic leg up to the hassock.

"Social services and the cops busted the kid's father but they couldn't find his mother. Even the Satanic connection was true. All true. Celeste, though, imagined the mother was the grand witch of the Satanic cult, hiding out, and she put everybody she didn't like into that cult, and everybody she did like was in danger of that cult. Truth was, the kid's mother had been toiling in the kitchen at Safeway until the demons in her head told her to drink some Drano and call it a day.

"Some of young Victor Merck's few personal things fell into Celeste's hands: pictures, school things, drawings. She constructed in her mind the image of an extraordinary boy, a boy full of courage and grit and wisdom and love, a boy who could be an inspiration for millions. And he might have been, really, but we'll never know, because the real Danny died in the hospital.

"Celeste was devastated. Her heart had been touched, and she in turn had touched real life, real emotions, and tragic events. She didn't like it. It didn't have to be that way. She simply refused to let him die. She renamed him Danny and gave him a voice. She talked to him and kept him alive in her imagination. She was good with voices. I'm guessing she'd lived with a number of imaginary friends before. Now, she imagined a wedding and an adoption. She imagined nursing the boy, never quite to full health but to the next day, and the next day, and the next.

"She inherited this house when your father died, so living alone in here she was prone to let her imagination take her where it would, her and her new imaginary husband and their sick imaginary little boy. You were off in the Army and your successful brother was a bit embarrassed by her, so he kept his contact to a minimum. But she told you both of the change in her life, even told some of the few people she knew about it. Life was a struggle, but what more noble struggle than to keep a boy alive and provide him with as much happiness at the end as she could? What a woman!"

What was keeping me there, in that cramped little living room? Was it his self-satisfied smile, his smirk, which should have been mine? I was the one, after all, who was unraveling Celeste's spun-up world and his complicity in it.

I browsed the spines of the books jamming the home-made shelves.

"Celeste is some kind of reader, ain't?"

"Always was."

"Yeah. The printed haven."

"People never saw how special she was," he said, and I was relieved to have him say anything. "Not our dad or our older brother. Even I couldn't see it, then. All anyone ever saw was the obesity, the weirdness, but when I came back from Iraq, what was left of me, she made whole again. She made me want to be back in the world again."

"Okay. But what world is that?"

He wouldn't say.

"She was a reader and, of course, a wannabe writer," I said. "She spent practically all her time in this room, sur-rounded by all these books, reading and writing and sending her stories out, only to have them come back, rejected and un-appreciated. Isn't that the way it was?"

He didn't say.

"She was also an insomniac, up most of the night. She'd always written fan letters to authors and once in a while got a return letter of polite but distant gratitude for her interest. But when she read about an author she admired who was dying of complications from AIDS, she wrote him a long heartfelt letter, this time as 'Danny.' What writer could resist responding to a precocious little boy who was also dying of AIDS and putting up a brave front? He even gave the boy his home telephone number and urged him to call if he needed to talk.

"Celeste was thrilled. She couldn't wait to call him, but she couldn't talk to him as herself. She had to call as a sick little boy. She was already having conversations with her imaginary boy, so she had the prepubescent voice down.

"She talked to the famous author about a history of cruelty and ritualized abuse, a history told to her by the real boy. But she told it in the first person. The writer and Danny became support for each other. They talked daily. The writer urged Danny to write down his stories. He arranged for Make-A-Wish Foundation to give the boy a computer and printer. Celeste got to work.

"She sent chapters to him. He was moved by what he read and introduced Danny, by phone, to his own agent and editor, both of whom adored the boy and do to this day, though they don't hear from him as often as they used to. Their prayers are with him as he endures, they think, an experimental protocol in France.

"The book was going to be published. Hoo-ray. At last, Celeste had become a professional writer. Kind of.

"Meanwhile, in Iraq, your Hummer cruises the horizon like a duck in a shooting gallery, and . . . well, your nation is grateful for your service and sorry for your loss, have a nice life. It's a bitch. After months of pain and rehabilitation, you're cut loose. Your wife had long past Dear Johned you." I saw his eyes go up. "Yeah, I know about the ex-wife. So the Army and the war are over for you. You're pretty messed up in a few different ways and you have no place to go. Who said, 'Home is the place where, when you have to go there, they have to take you in'?"

"Robert Frost. 'Death of the Hired Hand.' "

"I knew that. So you came here to read and sort it all out, sleeping, when you could, on this sofa. All in all, not a good time, but a necessary period of adjustment. I try to imagine the moment you realized your sister was a psycho. But the better moment had to be when you decided, what the hell, I'm a psycho, too. It doesn't much matter."

A risky but calculated jab. If I had to, I could beat him to the door. But he didn't flinch. Maybe being called a psycho was not that great an insult.

"Your deployment in Iraq taught you that nothing was real, so what the hell? You jumped into the hoax, playing the role of live-in doctor. I mean, what other role could you play? Since you were a medic in the Army you have a pretty workable knowledge of the field. The rest you can wing with Google."

"You've got a little lesion just below your jaw hinge there," he said, pointing. "You ought to have it looked at. Could be a basal cell carcinoma. Could be a melanoma."

There were no mirrors in the room, and it was all I could do not to search it out with my finger.

"I live in Seattle, who needs sunblock?"

"Very high rate of skin cancer up here. You wouldn't think so, but."

I knew I didn't have any lesion. I would have noticed it. Wouldn't have I? My throat was drying up, but I was not going to ask for a drink, and he wasn't going to offer me one. I pressed on.

"Thanks for the diagnosis. You want to hear mine?"

"It's up to you."

"The book is released and, I don't know, at that point it might have been just a giggle, a stunt well-pulled, but I have a feeling that Celeste has no sense of humor. I think she is always serious. Danny was a living thing to her. Just because he wasn't real didn't make it a hoax, not in her head. It had to be a mixed surprise to start getting interview requests from some newspapers, and then from media all over the country. People were moved by the tragic yet life-affirming story of this little boy.

"I have Danny on cassette saying how he hates it when people call him an inspiration, but, c'mon, nobody hates being an inspiration. Celebrities start calling. Oprah is mad for him. Major league baseball players say hi to him during pregame on-air interviews. Television sitcom stars call him up just to tell him to hang in there. People send T-shirts and coffee mugs. Famous writers dote on him, giving him generous blurbs. He becomes this wonder boy, half oracle, half guru, and totally and necessarily reclusive.

"No one can bask in his physical glow. He's the boy in the bubble. A sneeze down the street could kill him. Okay, the AIDS, that's bad, but it's the respiratory complications, the onset of TB, and the shingles, and the stroke he had, and the loss of his leg—was that your idea?—the removal of his spleen, his thirty-six broken bones, the syphilis—stage two—and the constant high fevers, and then the loss of an eye and the fear of losing the other one. Real doctors who hear of his symptoms are astounded. Where does this little boy, arrested in prepuberty, find the strength to go on living? In reality, the prototype, the little boy who called Celeste, couldn't go on living. He couldn't make it, he was too broken—and he had a lot less wrong with him than the imaginary Danny.

"But nobody questions anything. One telephone talk

with Danny and they're believers. The book is selling well and HBO comes calling. They hire a top screenwriter and want to make a movie of Danny's story. The screenwriter becomes a surrogate father to the boy. Now, this screenwriter is no pushover. He's a tough guy in a tough business, something of a survivor himself, but Danny melts his heart. Broken now, I'm guessing, if he's still alive.

"You jump in and become Alex's pal and medical adviser. Celeste works him, too. Why? Well, you can speak for yourself, but I'm betting she fell in love with him. Celeste falls in love with everybody, real or not. This relationship, all of you with Alex Krapp, becomes so rich that if Alex hadn't disappeared, here's the new scenario: The father, Bob, off there in Iraq would no longer be needed. He could die a hero, leaving Celeste a bereaved widow. No, too easy to verify. No, Celeste would take on a new role as an abandoned woman with a terminally ill child. She would be divorced from her short-lived marriage to a man who couldn't handle the pressures of looking after such a sick child.

"I'm not a shrink, but I can smell a major transference when it goes down. Why imagine a man in Iraq when you have a real one in LA? Alex, who is not naturally equipped for this sort of thing, tries to console Celeste while still sinking most of his energies into comforting Danny, putting him to sleep at night, holding him in his virtual arms. Celeste is flown to LA and everybody there really likes her, and she really likes Alex. He has that certain something. Even I had a little crush on him. Where will it end? Why does it have to?

"I'll tell you why. Most literary hoaxes fall over the same trip wire: they become too successful. Clifford Irving and his bogus Howard Hughes autobiography, James Frey, the Hitler diaries, J.T. LeRoy, the San Francisco hustler, and now little

Danny, the inspirational victim of Satanic abuse. You can't aim for a middling success. If a book takes off, it takes off, and you gotta ride with it. You and Celeste handled it very well, and she always had a safe out if someone got too close to the truth. She could kill off Danny, have a tearful memorial, and the rest is history. Only guess what? And you should have seen this coming. Celeste can't kill off Danny. Not ever. She's his mother! His creator! She'd kill herself first, but don't worry, I'm pretty sure she won't. I don't know where she is, but I know she has no remorse. Who got hurt? She thinks the boy was a blessing to all who talked to him. He wasn't real, he was better than real."

33

I STOOD AT THE MANTEL AND PICKED UP A FRAMED PICTURE of two small boys, their arms around each other's shoulder. Pals, with that special bond that only young boys have. I knew that one of them was dead and one was making his way through life. I felt a hot flash coming on. I tried to talk through it.

"As Danny became more of a public figure, only one person doubted him. Eve Gosler. Something early on in this story kicked off her bullshit detector and she convinced her editor to let her run with it. She's a good reporter, or she used to be.

"She started digging and couldn't find any records. No papers, no witnesses, nothing to support the existence of this young writer. She must have checked with the AMA, as I did, and learned there was no Doctor Victor D'Amato on the rolls. What did you tell her, Vic, that you were in the witness protection program?"

He wouldn't testify.

"Let's say all the names were changed and all the records

were sealed, as Celeste claimed, to protect everyone from hordes of Satanists determined to commit mayhem against anyone associated with a little boy who was at death's door anyway. Let's say all that. Why hasn't anyone come forward to say, I was that kid's teacher, I went to school with that kid, I treated that kid in the hospital. Seattle's not that big a place. An extraordinary kid with a horror tale like Danny's doesn't pass unnoticed. Why didn't his best friend Perry come forward? He could have supported the story. Ah, as the book tells us, Perry died tragically of a drug overdose while Danny was in the hospital. Well, he wasn't named Perry and he's never used drugs."

I turned the picture toward Vic. The hot flash was on me now, and I was raising my voice with impatience. "This is Victor Merck and his best friend, Ernie McCloskey, who is alive and working for United Parcel."

I opened the top two buttons and fanned myself with the picture. I turned around twice, as though there were any way out of it, someplace to elude it. I leaned one hand against the mantel and lowered my head.

"What's the matter with you?" Vic asked.

"Hot flash. Jesus, take me now."

"Try an eighth of a teaspoon of Maca with ten milligrams of pregnenolone in the morning."

"Write it down," I gasped.

He did. He had a pad next to the phone.

"It's homeopathic," he said.

"Son of a bitch," said I, as the thing passed through me and went wherever it goes after it's had its way with me.

Vic said, calmly, "Think of it as a reoccurring momentary cleansing of toxins."

I had to admit, he had a pretty good bedside manner.

"Not true," he added, "but it's easy to visualize and might help."

I took the note he handed me and stuck it into a pocket.

"Can't be any worse than what I already see it as: the firing up of the jets to push me beyond the pull of gravity."

I put the picture back on the mantel.

"Anyway," I said, fully recovered, "HBO hears of *Vanity Fair*'s investigation and starts getting cold feet. They still owe Danny a hundred grand, and all he has to do to get it and to see the movie of his life is to risk one minute with a man who loves him. Alex. But that didn't happen, never could happen. That's when Alex hired me."

"I can't believe he did that," said Vic. "That was a betrayal."

"He hired me not to prove that Danny didn't exist, but to prove that he *did*. He loved that imaginary boy. He believed in him. He wanted to protect him. He wasn't worried about his career. A derailed project at HBO was not going to affect his career. He just had to know that he wasn't nuts. He had to know that the boy he'd been talking to daily for over a year, with whom he'd bonded as a father bonds to a son, that a boy who made him laugh and cry and sing and see the good in life was, you know, a real person. He wanted everybody to know that Danny was what he knew him to be. How could he be otherwise? How could a phantom get so deep into his heart, how could he be no more than a faked voice of a fat psycho?"

"Watch it," said Vic, in that whiskey bass, and I thought that I'd better, that I should not so easily assume I was in charge. Calling *him* a psycho was one thing; calling his sister a fat psycho might be quite another.

"I apologize. Usually I could care less. Anyway, we're

coming to the end. HBO sweated the effects of an exposé in *Vanity Fair*. Eve was working the phone, talking to the principal players. The publisher, editor, agent, and Alex were stonewalling her. To do anything else, they thought, would be a betrayal of the wonder boy. But you and Celeste couldn't be more cooperative. Even Danny talked to her—over the phone, of course. I've never personally talked to Danny, so I can't guess what happens when you do, but it has to be some kind of magic. And if you love Danny you love Celeste and Vic, too, is the pattern. Again, I don't know what that was like, but obviously Eve flipped, in more ways than one.

"She's what, thirty-seven, -eight? Living alone in an overpriced apartment on the Upper West Side of New York, looking into other people's lives, hustling stories, going home alone. Parents and friends wondering if she'll ever meet a man, and her wondering herself, because no matter how rewarding it is to see your name in print, it's not enough.

"She's been talking to you on the phone a lot and something starts up. She wants to see you in person, and you agree, because, let's face it, supporting Celeste in her hoax has got to be wearisome, and Eve sounds so nice on the phone. And not bad in person, either. Cute blonde, great figure. You meet her and there's some chemistry, some real feelings, but you try to cut it short. Is it because you prefer men, or that you don't want to blow the whole fraud, or that you don't want to involve Eve in all of this insanity? Whatever, it didn't work. You both fall."

I could see in his face that I had it right. He wasn't smirking now.

"At some point you had to bring her home to meet the family. I'm sure it took some convincing for Celeste to take that chance. To tell you the truth, I can't even imagine how that went down, but at the end of it, Eve is willing to accept a different reality, in order to be with you. It was her fate."

I wanted to ask him how Eve turned into Celeste, physically. Was she emulating her, transforming herself to take Celeste's place? How can someone get so big so fast? I wanted to ask but didn't.

"Listening to the cassettes," I said, "one thing struck me. Danny was supposed to be terribly sick, at death's door. You wouldn't expect him to have much of an appetite, but he spent a lot of time talking about food, about pizza, pasta, and gooey desserts. Even a healthy boy doesn't preoccupy himself with food so much, unless he has an eating disorder."

He looked up from his easy chair. I stopped pacing.

"So are you done?" he asked. "Have you unloaded?"

"Pretty much. I have one question, though. Why? Why did she do it? It wasn't for money. Alex and others offered her money for medical bills, but she told everyone they were well-covered under Bob's imaginary GI insurance. So if it's not money, what's left? It's got to be love, the best kind, rich with attention, sympathy, respect, admiration, all things due a heroine in a fantasy."

"Was that a question?"

"I guess I answered it. So I'll ask another. Where is she, Vic?"

"I don't know. She's met a man."

"I thought she had a man, the one on the top-secret mission in Iraq."

"You didn't know? Divorced. Bob couldn't handle the pressure."

"Ah, as I predicted. And Danny? What happens to him?"

"France. When he's released from the hospital, he'll go to live with them."

"Them?"

"Celeste and her new love."

"Jesus, I'm getting a splitting headache. And what about you, where will you go?"

"Dunno. Why do I have to go anywhere?"

I shook my head still another time, trying to clear it. I wondered what I would do with the rest of the day. Maybe drink Sapphire Blue Martinis at Brasa.

"Who's this man Celeste has found?"

"You don't know?" asked Vic.

"No, why should I?"

"I thought maybe your boss might have mentioned it."

"Alex knows the guy?"

"Alex is the guy."

I put my hand over my mouth, stifled a little laugh. "Excuse me," I said, "I was picturing Celeste on the back of Alex's Harley."

"Couple of kids in love," said Vic, "off to start a new life. Wish them well."

"So she did it for love?"

"Why should she be any different?"

"And she's found love."

"Apparently."

"Not with Alex, though, that part can't be true."

What was I saying? None of it was true, and as far as I knew, Alex was dead. Or still missing.

It made me a little queasy to imagine it. Okay, you usually fall in love with the person who turns your heart inside out, but not like this.

The phone rang. There was a wireless receiver on the table next to Vic. He answered it, then said, with an uplift in his spirits, "Hey, buddy, how're you doing?" He finally got to his feet. His whole attitude changed.

I could hear only his half of the conversation.

"Don't worry about it. Are you eating?"

I got a tingling on the back of my neck. Not the good kind.

"Good, good man. Hey, I got those books you wanted. Amazon is gonna ship directly to you. . . . Well, that's kind of interesting. We have an unexpected visitor . . . a private detective Alex hired. . . . Hold on."

He turned to me. "What's your name again?"

"Quinn."

He spoke back into the telephone. "That's the one. She's got it all figured out. . . . You sure? Okay, hold on."

Vic handed the phone over to me.

At first, I didn't want to take it. This place was like a vortex. I didn't want to get sucked in. I was already crazy enough, for me. But take it I did, and said, "Hello?"

I heard that reedy, frail prepubescent voice. It had become familiar to me from listening to Krapp's cassettes.

"Hello, Quinn. Poppa told me you prefer to be called just Quinn."

"He did, huh?"

"I feel like I know you. Poppa has talked so much about you."

"Really? Now, why would he do that?"

"We talk about everything."

"The only marching orders I had, and they were solid, is that you never find out about me."

"Secrets are so destructive."

"You're the expert, Celeste."

"Poppa couldn't keep it from me. When he told me he had hired a detective, he was in tears. I cried, too, and then I forgave him. Forgiveness is such a wonderful remedy. I made a joke about the whole thing. I told him when you take your surveillance pictures to get my good side."

"I would have, but you can't take pictures of someone who doesn't exist."

"Quinn, Quinn . . ."

"Yeah, right."

I've been *Quinn, Quinn*ed before.

"Of course I exist. You're talking to me right now."

"I'm talking to you, but you're not a sick boy in a hospital in France. That poor boy died in a hospital in Seattle. He was the one who suffered the abuse that you exploited, the one who finally ran away and called the hotline. I've interviewed his father and I know his brother, sad to say."

"Poppa told me that you're recently divorced."

It was like I hadn't said a thing.

Damn, though, it gave me a jolt to know that Alex really had talked about me to Celeste, talked to the object of an investigation about the detective he'd hired. If he were with me now, I'd have popped him one with the phone.

"Remember your ex-husband, when you'd talk to him in the morning before going to work, and then you'd talk to him during the day, on the phone, and then in the evening when he came home late from work. Wasn't he a slightly different person each time you talked to him?"

"Maybe, but at the end of the day I could look at him and touch him and know he was my husband."

Sometimes, though, after he had been with Esther and then come home to me, he really wasn't the same person, and although I thought he was my husband, he wasn't anymore.

"He was never your husband," said the small fragile voice, as though reading my mind. "He was just a man living with you while looking for someone else. Some people are so tied into reality that the truth eludes them. *Seeing* becomes impossible for them."

I stopped listening to her ruminations about truth, reality, and perception. Not because I knew I was on the phone with an unbalanced woman. No, I was distracted by a voice in the background. It was a man's voice, from somewhere in the same room. I couldn't understand what he was telling her, if indeed he was even talking to her. He was speaking French.

About the Author

ANNE ARGULA was born in Shenandoah, Pennsylvania, and raised there and in Ringtown. She currently lives in Seattle, Washington. This is her third novel in the Quinn series.